The Revenge of Tirpitz

M L Sloan

pokey
hat

First published in 2016 by Pokey Hat

Pokey Hat is an imprint of Cranachan Publishing Limited

Copyright © M. L. Sloan 2016

www.michellesloan.co.uk

@michlsloan

ISBN: 978-1-911279-06-8

www.cranachanpublishing.co.uk

@cranachanbooks

cranachan

For Donald

Contents

Prologue: Race for The Shetland Bus   1
1 Scalloway Museum   8
2 The Burial Site   10
3 Lunch   12
4 Secrets at School   17
5 Tirpitz   21
6 Nightmares   26
7 The German   29
8 The Chase   33
9 The Werewolves   39
10 Hans   43
11 Friends and Enemies   48
12 The Visit   54
13 Union Jack   59
14 The Resistance   63
15 The Great Escape Part 1   68
16 Bike Ride   74
17 Radar   78
18 The Great Escape, Part 2   85
19 The Secret Room   90
20 Stockfish   95
21 The Mountain Sami   100
22 Aboard The Northern Light   105
23 The Cave   109
24 Cave Diggers   113
25 The Agent   118
26 The Dream   124

27 Kristoffer   128
28 Sabotage   133
29 The Gathering Storm   137
30 Sabotage Part 2   140
31 Sabotage Part 3   144
32 Squall Line   148
33 Tirpitz Day   151
34 The Race   155
35 Struggles at Sea Part 1   160
36 Hans on the Run   164
37 Struggles at Sea Part 2   168
38 Erik's Father   171
39 Farewell   176
40 Welcoming Party   180
41 The Reunion   184
42 The Cellar   190
43 The Suitcase   194
44 Gold Hunt   198
45 Erik and Olde   202
46 Finn and Gus   207
47 The Final Battle   211
48 The Sea Eagle   214
49 Havørn   217

Glossary   222
Author's Note   223
Acknowledgements   224
About the Author   225

PROLOGUE

Race for The Shetland Bus

NORWAY 1944

'Take this gun,' said the agent. 'You will need it. There are Nazis everywhere.'

He signalled to outside the hut where the last wisps of the storm were trailing away. The hut stood isolated, clinging to the snow-smattered hillside; and now the chill of the night had taken hold.

The man took the revolver and nodded. He understood.

'I've radioed the crew of the boat—it's called *Havørn*,' continued the agent.

'Does the skipper know about me? And the crew?' the man asked, tentatively.

The agent stared at the man before him, perched uncomfortably on the wooden chair. He looked weary; one arm was strapped tight against his chest in a sling. His face was tired and tense; haunted even. Deep lines were etched into a permanent frown. He clearly hadn't washed for days. His clothes were torn.

The agent nodded. 'Yes, Olsen radioed us and passed on everything. The skipper is expecting you. You will rendezvous with *Havørn* at Reine in one hour. You must

1

follow the road at the bottom of the hill for three miles until you reach the harbour.' He paused then added, 'Be safe. *Havørn* cannot wait for you.'

The man nodded. He stood, his body cold and stiff, his slung arm aching and opened the door to the hut. Outside, though the landscape was drenched in darkness, the moon was trying to peer out from behind swift-moving clouds. The snow-capped peaks shone out in the flitting snatches of moonlight. Somewhere there was a screech. Was it an owl? Or the cry of a sea eagle? The man took a deep breath and looked back into the hut.

'Goodbye,' he said to the agent. 'And thank you.' He turned and plunged himself down the hillside, into the hostile zone.

He'd found his way up there earlier in the day, but then he'd had the help of a guide. Now he was stumbling blindly in the dark. Alone.

The man had been on the run for days now. Sometime earlier (had it been last night? Or the night before that? He had no concept of time) some fishermen had rescued him from the wreckage of the sinking boat he'd been travelling on. His skipper, despite their best efforts, was taken by the sea.

By remarkable fortune, the fishermen had known the skipper, known he was helping the Resistance. And after hauling the man from the freezing waters, they had offered to take him on to the Lofoten islands where a guide—a local—had intelligence of the whereabouts of the agent. Together they had crept carefully, out of sight, to avoid unwelcome attention, dodging Nazis, trekking for miles.

But now, negotiating the hillside, he had never felt so alone. Fear began to smother him. He stopped his descent and listened to his breath, loud and uneven, his heart pounding. He steadied himself and waited for his pulse to calm. The moon broke through and he could just make out in the distance the snaking curve of a road. Fear put to one side, he picked up his pace. He could not afford to miss the rendezvous.

The man gathered momentum as he sped down the hillside towards the road, his broken arm clutched tight to his body in its sling, the other arm helping to keep his balance. His feet slipped on the scree but still he ran on, the road nearly within reach. With desperation mounting as he ran, he became more daring, his speed almost out of control. But he was nearly there! He leapt wildly now into the dark unknown, until his luck ran out. He missed his footing and fell, rolling and spinning down the craggy hillside. The rocks tore at his clothes and his flesh and he tumbled over and over until he landed with a thud. At least he had made it to the bottom of the hill. He wrenched his body over and groaned. Blood spilled from his nose, his limbs ached. But something made him freeze. His ears filled with a sound that terrified him—a car—coming this way. He immediately hauled himself to the side of the road to scurry into the bushes. The chequered moonlight soon illuminated two Nazi vehicles—a truck, and a motorbike with sidecar—speeding where he had, moments ago, been lying. In the truck, two rows of men sat in the back face to face, with straight backs, hats silhouetted.

When he was sure they had gone, he eased himself out of hiding and set off again. But running became limping as cloying pain took hold of his right leg as he tried to pick up the pace.

He wore no watch so now relied on calculated judgements of time. Each few steps were allocated as a minute, two minutes—this continued and accumulated. Before long, he was up to half an hour. Beads of sweat formed on his head and neck. Doubts flashed through his mind.

He wasn't going to make it.

The darkness ahead was confusing. The clouds now covered the moon and as he waded on through the black he felt disorientated. Direction was based on the road underfoot. But he seemed to see a light in the far off distance—was it the harbour? A house with no blackout? It now appeared to be several tiny lights, moving and dancing. And then he realised—it was the Nazi troops. They had stopped up ahead, and they were smoking cigarettes. The soft, shielded glow of the vehicle headlights revealed the outline of steep rocky hillsides bordering each side of the road. There was no way past them; he was trapped. A plan quickly formed in his mind. It was reckless but, to have a chance of making the rendezvous point, he would have to take a tremendous risk.

The man wiped the blood that had trickled out of his nose with the back of his sleeve. He pulled his hat further down over his ears and set off, walking directly towards the vehicles. The running engine and men's banter masked the sound of his footsteps as he approached the truck. He crept silently, tapping his pocket to make sure the gun was there and carefully moved along the side of the truck, all the time listening to the prattle of the men's conversations. He reached for the handle of the door and with a click opened it, slipping inside. Without wasting another moment, he crunched the gear stick forward. Before the Nazis realised what had happened, his foot was down hard on the accelerator and the truck screeched forward, the door still swinging. The shouts of the startled men could be heard over the grinding of the engine as the truck roared into the night.

It was hard to manoeuvre the steering wheel with one arm in the sling, and he had to use his knee to steady it as he reached over to change gears. The truck swerved wildly, and with a quick glance to his rear view mirror, he could see a single headlight. The motorbike was after him. It wouldn't take long to catch him as the truck was heavy and sluggish. He pressed his foot to the floor and squinted, focussing intently on what he could make out of the road ahead. How much further?

Suddenly, a sign appeared in the low glow of the headlights: there was a sharp bend in the road. With a screech of tyres, he swerved too late. His able arm grabbed frantically at the steering wheel, but the truck went crashing off the road into a ditch. He was thrown forward, hitting his head sharply. With no time to review his injuries, desperation spurred him on. He clambered out of the vehicle, and set off running blindly into the black of the night. He had no idea of the direction he was heading; there was nothing to guide him.

The sound of the heaving motorbike engine was now

close behind him. He swung round to look. The dim headlight seemed to freeze as the engine died. They too were on foot, running closely behind him, scrabbling and shouting.

The clouds shifted and a bright moon lit up the scene ahead, an intervention that would propel everything to a conclusion. The man could now make out the glimmer of the sea. Waiting in the tiny harbour was a single fishing boat: *Havørn*.

His path was clear—it could only be a hundred feet or so! The ricochet of a piercing gunshot echoed into the night. As the moon had lit up his route, so too had it revealed his location to the agitated Nazis. The man reached into this pocket, and with one swift action, swung round and took a shot. Instantly, he was met with another shot. It was two—perhaps three—against one. He shot again and another bullet whizzed past him. This one he heard in his ear as it flew by. They were closer now; their aim more accurate. The hillside dipped and he realised his own stuttering pace was slowing when the heavy breathing of one of the Nazis grew ever closer. He took a chance, swung round again and aimed. This time, he shot three times in quick succession. He heard a low scream. One was down! He stumbled on and mentally counted the bullets he'd used. He had one left.

Havørn was close now, but as he approached, something wasn't right. Wiping the sweat (or was it blood?) from his forehead, he stared out to sea. Was the boat moving? They must have heard the gunshots and decided to leave before it was too late.

'NO! Wait!' he yelled. His shout sounded pathetic in the vastness of the space. 'Wait!' he shrieked again, his voice cracking and breaking. 'I'm here! I've made it!'

Gunshots once more, and again he could feel the very ripples in the air as the bullets sped by. But mercifully, their aim this time was poor.

Now the harbour, with its pier spiking into the sea, was before him. *Havørn* was edging out, and so he had no choice. He set his mind and his body to sprint, ignoring the shooting pains in his limbs. And with one final push he took a leap off the edge, into the air—both feet thrust forward.

He grabbed onto the railing and outstretched arms hauled him over and onto the safety of the deck. Another gun shot rang out—this time someone from *Havørn* was covering them.

He could barely breathe. Each gasp of air ached. He tried to speak.

'I'm Hans,' he exhaled, coughing and rasping. 'You were expecting me, no?'

The skipper nodded. 'Yes,' he said calmly. 'We were hoping you would make it. And now, Hans, we're on our way.' He paused and added, 'We're on our way to Shetland.'

CHAPTER ONE

Scalloway Museum Opening Ceremony
THE SHETLAND ISLANDS, SCOTLAND 2014

'Ladies and Gentleman, I am delighted to introduce the Prime Minister of Norway.'

Applause rippled around the room and a row of small children at the front enthusiastically waved little Norwegian flags. Then a hush. The Prime Minister stood and stepped up to the microphone.

'Seventy years ago,' she began, 'courage was simply part of everyday life. The War created super-heroes. Not the kind that fly or have special powers,' she directed this to the younger children at the front. 'No, it was their bravery, in the face of Nazi oppression, that made ordinary people take extraordinary risks for the freedom of our countries.' She paused and looked around the room at the rows of faces, young and old. 'This museum is a wonderful tribute to those people who gave their lives for our future. Norway and the Shetland Islands shall be forever bonded by our shared history, by our awe of those who were part of the incredible 'Shetland Bus' operations. Manned by brave, selfless souls, small fishing boats sailed in perilous conditions to and fro across the sea, keeping a vital lifeline open for our occupied nation. I am honoured, as Prime Minister of Norway, to be invited here today. And without further ado, I declare this museum "open"!' She pulled the cord on a small pair of blue curtains, revealing a bronze plaque on the wall.

Once again clapping rang out. The children cheered.

8

Lightbulbs flashed and television cameras scanned happy faces around the room.

The camera focused in on veterans. An old man in a wheelchair on the very back row raised his hands slowly to join the applause. With each mechanical clap an image flashed in his mind; an image from seventy years ago.

He remembers. He remembers the war and he remembers his journey from Norway to Shetland.

Chapter Two

The Burial Site

Tromsø, Norway 2014

With his hands clamped tightly in his pockets, the old man stood at the shoreline. Bitter, freezing winds whipped his craggy face. He closed his eyes momentarily and replayed the scenes that had been broadcast live on Norwegian TV from Shetland. The camera focused on their Prime Minister opening the museum. But it had also scanned the crowd and lingered on the people there watching the ceremony.

Lingered on him!

Seventy years had passed, but that old man at the back of the room sitting clapping... it was unmistakably him. Not dead after all. All this time alive. Alive! He couldn't believe it. Living in Shetland!

He looked grimly at the water at his feet, murky and frothing; fragments of ice were turning it to a thick soup, full of secrets. Small waves pushed and pulled rhythmically towards his toes. For a moment, he was lost in it, trance-like. He cast his eyes downward to the objects lying on the belt of seaweed, a foot back from the water. Here lay lumps of sea-worn driftwood, fragments of faded plastic and bottle tops. Kicking a worn boot through the debris, he walked further along, eyes scanning carefully. How much could be left, he mused? Sordid souvenir hunters had been diving, stripping the seabed of these last pieces. And this, a burial site! Unprotected from the vultures! The old man turned to spit a mouthful of hatred and bile onto the rocks, when something caught his eye.

Lying almost hidden amongst seaweed and moss was a rusty prong. His gnarled fingers, red and swollen from the cold, poked and prodded, heaving and tearing it from the clutches of the overgrown moss. What was it this time? A bit of panelling perhaps? He gently caressed its flaking surface. A rivet sat tight in its hole, soldered by rust for eternity. The old man closed his eyes and drifted, imagining the moment that metal pin was hammered into place. Someone had taken pride in that fixing. Whomever he was had been part of her creation! Anger surfaced in his gullet. Acid bile rose in his throat. What use had it all been? For it to be obliterated, smashed to pieces, her men trapped and drowning inside as she sank?

He closed his eyes and in his mind he could see the mighty ship entering the fjord. And now all that was left were shards of her carcass resurfacing seventy years on. His eyes flashed open. He had waited long enough. Time may be running out, but it was never too late. Never too late.

Tirpitz would have her revenge!

CHAPTER THREE

Lunch

LERWICK, THE SHETLAND ISLANDS 2014

The very sight of an old person eating was enough to make Finn feel queasy. There was something about the way the folds of flesh on their neck flapped back and forth with each chew. It would put anyone off their own food. He always had to be careful not to retch; having lunch with his great-grandfather today would be torture.

But, as always, what hit him as soon as he walked through the door of Bay View Care Home, was not just the stifling heat, but the smell. It was a nauseating mix of something sweet, sweaty almost and, of course, disinfectant. He buried his face in his hoodie. Anna, his gran, must have noticed his disgust as she turned to him and frowned.

'Why are you hiding your face, Finn?' she complained. 'And pull back your hood for goodness' sake. Come on, we need to find Olde.'

Finn rolled his eyes. That wouldn't take long. It wasn't as if he could go far. The residents (or 'inmates') were under lock and key in this hellhole. Finn pointed towards the main lounge and shrugged. 'There's Olde there,' he said. "Olde" was short for "Oldefar": the Norwegian for great-grandfather. His proud family were keen to keep his nationality alive and in the present. And besides, Finn always remarked that he was an 'oldie' so it was a perfect fit.

Sure enough, when they wandered in, there he was, sitting

in a large circle of other old people. Finn looked around the room. He found it all a wee bit depressing. Their eyes drooped, some nodded continuously.

But Olde was engrossed in his newspaper, wearing headphones, unaware of anyone else—he was lost in the music, his foot tapping.

'Morning!' said Anna over-enthusiastically, lifting up an earphone. 'And how are we today?'

The old man, now in his early nineties but still with a full head of pure white hair, was wiry and sharp-minded. He didn't miss a trick. He immediately lowered his paper and snatched the headphones round the back of his neck.

'Why do you always say, "how are *we*"?' the old man snapped. 'We are not amused.' He eyed Finn cautiously and barked to his daughter, 'Is that boy on drugs? He's as white as a sheet!'

Anna rolled her eyes, and wheeled his chair around towards the door. 'No, of course not. Don't say such ridiculous things.'

'They all take drugs nowadays don't they? And sit in the dark playing computer games, shooting people. Or shooting up. That's what they say, isn't it?' said Olde, staring hard at Finn.

'We're not all like that, Olde,' Finn grunted, now feeling overwhelmed by the stifling warmth and the smell; he was beginning to feel sick.

'Oh well, at least I got your attention, eh Finn?' chuckled Olde. 'Got you talking!' He leant forward and gave Finn a wee tweak on his knee. Finn twisted the corner of his mouth into something of a smile and shook his head. He held the door for the wheelchair and they manoeuvred the old man into his room and opened the patio doors. The sun streamed in and a cool breeze freshened the stale air.

'Want a listen?' Olde offered his headphones up to Finn. They were connected to an ancient-looking portable CD player.

'Nah, you're alright, Olde,' Finn said, waving his hand away. 'Don't think it would be my kind of thing.'

'You're missing out; it's toe-tapping stuff,' said Olde. 'Jazz! The hip-hop of my day!'

'Now, what would we like for lunch today?' asked Anna briskly.

'How's school, Finn?' said Olde, ignoring his daughter.

Finn shrugged and gazed out of the window, with his arms folded as he slumped down in the chair.

Olde pushed him further, 'You'll have to speak up, boy. I didn't quite hear that.'

'I left school, Olde. I'm working with Dad now,' Finn said loudly. He paused, looking for a wave of recognition across his great-grandfather's face. 'I'm on the boat, with Dad and Gus.'

A trace of a smile flickered across the old man's shrivelled lips. He continued to stare at his great-grandson, his large eyes watery.

'Well! That's something, Finn. That is something. On the boat, eh?' He seemed vaguely impressed. He raised an eyebrow. 'Must be in your blood. But why aren't you out today?'

They were interrupted by a gentle knock at the door. Anna opened it. A uniformed arm handed her an envelope and a blue card of some description.

'That's the lunch menu,' said Anna, closing the door. 'And the post for you, Olde.'

Anna began to read the list from the menu while Olde took the envelope. His great-grandfather eyed the letter carefully. A strange look seemed to pass across his face. Finn frowned. Now, his great-grandfather's loose, saggy jaw tightened. He turned the envelope over to examine the address, then swiftly stuffed it down the side of his leg into the cushion of the wheelchair.

They ordered lunch. Finn was quietly repulsed at some of the options: 'Scotch Broth, Shepherd's Pie, Beef Olives,

Stovies.' He decided he would try to sit beside Olde at the table, so that he wouldn't have to actually look at him as he ate his soup. Soup! Of all things! It was sure to be dribbled everywhere. Finn chose a cheese sandwich and a packet of crisps; surely he could cope with that.

Anna chatted while Finn purposely looked out of the window as they ate. He counted each mouthful before swallowing. Olde was distracted and didn't always hear what was said. Although Finn was pretty certain he just zoned out when he was bored.

'We'll need to get that hearing aid adjusted,' shouted Anna.

Olde grunted. He had selective hearing and dropped into conversations when it suited him.

'What was your letter? Anything interesting?' asked Anna brightly.

'Nope,' replied Olde curtly. 'Nothing interesting at all.'

He reached for his cup but his hand shook violently. Finn looked properly at his great-grandfather for the first time since he'd arrived. Olde didn't normally shake so much. He tried to grasp the cup but instead knocked it over, spilling water all over the table. With a rush of napkins, they tried to stem the flow but it was too late. Finn and Anna jumped up, water instantly soaking their clothes.

'Damn!' shouted Olde.

'Oh dear!' Anna quickly tried to soothe. 'Don't worry, these things happen. I'll fetch a cloth.'

Anna sped out of the room.

'Your letter, Olde,' said Finn.

'What?' muttered Olde.

'The letter. You put it down there,' he said pointing to the inside of the wheelchair. 'Didn't it get wet?'

Olde awkwardly slid his fingers down and retrieved the letter. His hand shook.

The envelope was wet. He pushed his thumb into the flap on the back but the paper was dissolving fast and his gnarled fingers were awkward and slow.

'Open it boy! My hands are too old and clumsy. Do it quick before she comes back.'

Finn tore the soaking envelope and very carefully pulled out the letter inside. The ink was running but the words could clearly be made out.

Confusion spread across Finn's face. 'Olde? What does this mean? What's it all about?'

It was short and to the point:

I know what you did.

We know where you are.

Tirpitz will have her revenge.

There were footsteps in the corridor. Finn looked into Olde's panic-stricken face. A bony hand shot out, grabbed the soggy paper and stuffed it back into the depths of the wheel chair. He leaned forward and grasped Finn's knee with surprising strength, his murky eyes now wide and glaring.

'Now you know, you have to help me, boy! I am in great danger. We are all in great danger!'

Chapter Four

Secrets at School

Norway 1944

Erik carefully lifted the net curtain an inch with the end of his pen and lowered his head to gaze out of the window. From here in the old wooden school house, nestled high on the snow-speckled hillside, Erik had an uninterrupted view of the mouth of the fjord and out to the vast sea beyond. Sometimes, if he was really lucky, he could make out the shape of a sea eagle soaring high above the rocks, or the curious bob of a seal far out to sea, or the silhouette of a fishing boat: his father's perhaps. Although now light, a brooding gloom hung over the sky; a storm was beginning to whip up the coastline. Every so often, the wind would whistle and moan through the gaps in the window frame, billowing the thin lace curtains, drowning out the crackle and spit of the wood burner.

The door to the school room flew open, the wind caught its hinges and it slammed loudly against the wall. Everyone jumped, their concentration or dreams temporarily shattered. Freezing air blasted into the room, accompanied by a flurry of sleety rain, and pages caught by the sudden gust flew onto the floor. In shuffled Kristoffer. Heavily built and imposing, he surveyed the room, a half smile on his lips. He flicked his thick blonde hair casually out of his eyes.

'Late again, Kristoffer?' Mr. Olsen groaned. 'Come here, boy, and collect your exercise book.'

Unapologetic, Kristoffer slouched towards his teacher's desk to snatch up his jotter. He would get away with it, of course. Again. He was late just about every day of school and never received a punishment, other than a few stern words. His father was the community policeman and a Nazi supporter—a 'quisling'. Everyone was in fear of him and his snitching. Several innocent men had been reported at his whim and sent away, never to be seen again. Mr Olsen didn't dare punish his precious son Kristoffer, for fear he might end up in a concentration camp.

Erik sighed and looked down at his page and then at the blackboard in front of him. He attempted to continue with his German grammar, but it made no sense. Again his eyes were pulled to the sea behind the net curtains. Through the lace, he could see frothy white waves whipping and lashing. How Erik longed to toss his books into the sea, to spend the precious few hours of daylight exploring the shoreline with its caves and secrets.

Kristoffer now turned and walked slowly down the aisle of seats, throwing menacing glances to his classmates. He glared with his unflinching cold, blue eyes, but Erik held his stare until he had passed to settle himself in the seat behind him.

Erik noticed his friend, Magnus, at the far end of the classroom; he was clearly trying to get his attention. Magnus gave a flick of his head, his blonde hair flopping over to one side, and mouthed something to Erik with an excited gleam in his eyes. Erik frowned and gave his head a small shake of doubt. Magnus mouthed it again: two syllables. Then he tapped his watch. Erik shrugged—he still couldn't make out what his friend was trying to tell him. And he didn't want to draw attention to himself by continuing to stare. He reluctantly returned to his grammar, lifting his pen to scratch out the German words. Magnus should know better than to pass on information so openly, he thought to himself.

Magnus's father, Per Johansen, ran the local shop, but he was also a Resistance supporter, housing agents in the dead of night, brought in on fishing boats—some even from Scotland. Magnus had confided in Erik about the strange goings on at home; keeping secrets was a way of life now. If the Nazis found out, the consequences were unthinkable.

Erik felt a nudge at his knee and looked down. A small, folded piece of paper was thrust towards him. Erik followed the line of the outstretched arm to his nearest classmate and along the row, all the way to Magnus, who was now pretending to be engrossed in his work.

Erik reached down to grab the note, but another hand grabbed it first. He swung round to see Kristoffer grinning. He held the note in front of Erik's face and, as he reached forward to grab it, Kristoffer snatched it back again. Erik shot a look over to Magnus who was watching anxiously. Meanwhile, Olsen had his back to them and was writing on the blackboard. Quick as a flash, Erik whipped round and slapped Kristoffer's hand as hard as he could with his ruler. The sound of wood hitting flesh was startlingly loud.

Shocked, Kristoffer yelped and dropped the paper. Erik retrieved the note and slid it under his book. Olsen turned quickly to face the class. But all he could see was Kristoffer sucking the back of his hand. Olsen raised one eyebrow and then returned to conjugating German verbs on the board.

Erik knew he'd be for it as soon as the bell rang, but he wasn't going to worry about that now. The worst that would happen would be a beating from Kristoffer. He was pretty sure he wouldn't be bleating to the Nazis about a slap on the back of the hand.

Making sure he wasn't being watched, Erik slipped the paper under his palm. He opened the note carefully and slid it into his jotter. Then he casually turned the page to glance at it. Scrawled in Magnus's messy handwriting were three words that quickened his pulse.

Tirpitz is coming.

CHAPTER FIVE

Tirpitz

NORWAY 1944

Erik weighed up his options. He could either scarper out of the schoolhouse the minute they were dismissed and cycle home like the clappers, or he could face Kristoffer's beating. The other option, he supposed, was to hang back with Mr. Olsen and feign interest in some additional teaching. Olsen would never fall for that one and would send him packing. And bolting away from school would only prolong the inevitable. No. Erik decided he would face Kristoffer head on and take the punches. It would hurt, but how bad would it be really? A couple of black eyes?

'Right everyone, books closed. That is all for today,' announced Mr. Olsen. 'See you tomorrow, bright and early,' then added dryly, 'Kristoffer—*try* to set your alarm half an hour earlier.'

There was a flurry of movement. Chairs scraped on the floor, desk lids opened and slammed. With much shouting and laughter, the children exited the school house. Erik took a deep breath. This was it. He shut his book, placed it inside his desk and cautiously closed the lid. When he looked up the room was almost empty. Kristoffer must have quickly slipped past. He would be waiting outside, no doubt—ready to pounce.

Erik trudged out the door, a lamb to the slaughter. As he shuffled down the steps there was no sign of Kristoffer. Only Magnus stood, waiting.

'Where'd he go?' said Erik.

'You mean Kristoffer?' replied Magnus. 'He set off down the road at a fair pace.' Magnus bit his lip, as though to stop himself from saying something. Instead, he shook his head looking in the direction Kristoffer had gone.

'I thought he would be waiting to give me a pounding,' said Erik, relief flooding over him.

'No time for that right now. He's saving you for later. He'll have heard the news too from his rat of a father. C'mon, we've got to get down the hill,' urged Magnus.

Erik had momentarily forgotten about Magnus's note. *Tirpitz*, the great Nazi warship, was supposedly sailing into their fjord anytime and, as the light was fading, they would be best positioned down the hill by the water's edge to catch a glimpse of her. There had been many whisperings of *Tirpitz*. Sightings were reported and information on her whereabouts filtered through agents' secret radios up and down the coastline. Magnus's dad had heard she was coming to Tromsø, at the top of their fjord. There she would sit like a spider on her web. Waiting. The world was terrified of her presence.

Magnus jumped on the back of Erik's bike and they set off down the uneven track, their bones rattling inside their heads as they bounced along.

'Stop a minute, Erik!' shouted Magnus sharply in Erik's ear.

Erik gripped his brakes and the bike skidded to a halt.

'What?' groaned Erik.

'Sssshhhh!' Magnus whispered.

They were silent. Listening. At first, Erik couldn't understand what Magnus was so insistent about. There was the odd cry of a seagull or two. The wind whipped the waves near them. The old stunted, twisted trees near the coast waved and creaked.

But there was another layer of noise—a distant hum; it was rhythmical and pulsating like a heartbeat. There was something unnerving about this sound as it steadily crescendoed. Erik shivered. It was coming nearer, but as they looked out to sea there was nothing except the horizon ahead of them. The two boys wandered down the pebbly beach to the shore and waited, the pulse of the ship's engine in the distance.

And then they saw her. Edging around the corner, surrounded by an escort, a vast, malevolent black silhouette appeared in their fjord. The hum, now louder, echoed around the cliffs and hillsides of the narrow inlet as the imposing battleship powered menacingly towards them. Erik felt his mouth drop open. He'd never seen a ship this size before. With her massive guns spiked towards the heavens and a mast that seemed almost as tall as the mountains on either side, *Tirpitz* was truly terrifying. She cut through the frothing sea effortlessly, and passed the two stunned boys on the shoreline—ants dwarfed by her monstrous presence.

Neither boy spoke. They were quite still as she continued on up the fjord, leaving them dumbstruck. In her wake, the water still rippled and lapped like a writhing pool of poison. The steady beat of her engine faded into the night that now enveloped them.

Magnus spoke first.

'Hitler's beast,' he murmured quietly.

Erik nodded. He felt low; despondent, even. *Tirpitz* had filled him with dark despair. How were they ever going to win the war?

They set off, trudging back up the hill, taking turns to push the bike. It was tricky to see where they were going in the dark and they stumbled and cursed as they went. But there was no chatter; silence was better than acknowledging their fears. At the top of the hill they mounted the bike. But the path seemed somehow unfamiliar.

'Did we take the wrong turning somewhere?' said Magnus.

'No!' snapped Erik. 'I come here all the time. There's no way I would get this wrong.'

But as they continued, it dawned on Erik that perhaps the shock of seeing *Tirpitz* had confused him and they had indeed stumbled onto the wrong track.

'So, where are we?' said Magnus, sounding nervous.

Erik looked around. It was now pitch dark. He didn't want to show his anxiety, but he had no idea what path they were on.

'Let's just wander along here for a bit. I'm pretty certain it joins up with the top road to the village.' Erik feigned confidence so as not to frighten Magnus.

They struggled on, now on foot, but the path narrowed and became more of a sheep trail. Pushing the bike was becoming increasingly difficult.

'This is hopeless,' whined Magnus. 'I think we should turn back.'

This time it was Erik's turn to press his finger to his lips. 'Shhhhhh!'

The two boys stood silently in the dark: listening. But this time the distant sound they heard was music. Not just any music. They could distinctly hear the rhythmical beat of jazz.

Chapter Six

Nightmares

Lerwick, The Shetland Islands 2014

'Mrs. Anderson, could I possibly have a word?'

A nurse popped her head in the room as they were finishing their lunch. Finn hadn't a clue what was going on. He had felt a bit dazed as he'd chewed on his sandwich, mulling over the words in Olde's letter. Was it some kind of a joke? But surely it was a bit strange to target an ancient old man like Olde? Perhaps he had gone a bit funny in the head or something.

Anna jumped up, looking anxious, and left the room immediately.

'Olde?' said Finn.

The old man looked up wearily. His pallor had changed; he was grey.

'What's going on? What was that letter about?' Finn wished his older brother, Gus, was there. He would know what to say to Olde and how to act around his great-grandfather.

The old man turned and looked out of the window.

'It's not the first. Look in my wardrobe, inside my black shoe.'

Finn fumbled to open the door and looked inside. Tucked into the heel of Olde's shoe was a neat bundle of letters, bound together with a rubber band. There must have been around ten. Finn began to flick through them; the handwriting and format of each letter was identical. The messages were also similar in their threatening tone.

'When did these start coming?' he asked.

'A few months ago,' replied Olde.

'What do they mean? What is revenge of,' he looked closely at the document and over enunciated the word, '*Tir-pitz?*'

Olde stared at his great-grandson. He slumped a little and shook his head.

'Have you learned nothing of the war?'

Finn shrugged.

'Which war? Sorry, Olde. I didn't choose History at school,' Finn felt a bit embarrassed. 'We did some stuff about evacuees at primary school. That's WW2 right? And I know a peerie bit about the Shetland Bus, of course,' he shrugged. 'I dunno. It doesn't seem relevant now. Like, you know, I mean it was so long ago.'

'Relevant?' Olde said. 'Seems pretty relevant to me now!'

'Look, gran'll be back any minute,' said Finn. Getting into this kind of discussion wasn't helpful. 'What d'you want me to do with these? Surely we should take them to the police or something.'

Olde waved his hands. 'No, no police, boy,' he said. Then added, 'Do you have a car?'

'A car?' spluttered Finn. 'Eh, I've only just passed my test, Olde. There's no way Dad'll get me a car! Nope. Sorry, Olde. Definitely no car.'

'No car,' Olde repeated slowly. 'But you do have a boat—or at least access to one—don't you, boy?'

Finn stared at the old man. 'What? Yes. But wait, what's all this about?' He was beginning to feel a bit out of his depth when suddenly they were interrupted. Anna came rushing in. She looked a little flustered and her eyes were red. Finn quickly stuffed the letters into his back pocket. Olde flashed him a grateful half smile.

'Sorry about that. How are you getting along now?' said Anna. 'Shall we order some tea? Finn, pop along and ask for tea for three, will you?'

Olde turned back to the window. Finn shrugged and shuffled out of the room.

He ambled along the carpeted corridors, looking for someone to ask for tea, but had no luck. He headed back the way he'd come, but stopped right outside Olde's room. Gran was talking to Olde. Her voice sounded strained and a little high-pitched.

'I'm just worried about you, that's all. The nurse heard you. She heard you, well, crying out in your sleep. She said you were shouting and in some distress.'

'I've already told you,' Olde said, sounding irritated. 'It was a nightmare, Anna: pure and simple. For goodness' sake, it was nothing.'

'I'm just saying, is there something on your mind?'

There was a long pause. Finn wondered if he should walk in, but something made him hold back. Olde's voice ached with frustration.

'The deaths of a thousand men are on my mind. The deaths of a thousand of my comrades!'

Finn could hear his own breathing, as he stood pressed against the wall.

'And someone out there, after nearly 70 years, knows it was me!'

CHAPTER SEVEN

The German

NORWAY 1944

'We're not lost! I know where we are,' said Erik confidently. 'We must be near the German radar operators' billets.'

'But that's miles away from the village!' said Magnus.

'No, not the radar station. The operators stay in huts down this way. This must be it. Our road is further up the hill. We turned off the path too early.'

'Why are they playing that music?' said Magnus.

'Dunno,' answered Erik. 'Let's go and take a look.'

Erik gave Magnus a gentle push forward.

'C'mon Magnus,' he said with a smile. He knew his friend was anxious. 'They'll not see us! Let's find out what these Nazis get up to!'

The two boys crept forward towards the small wooden huts. Lights glowed and the music pulsated. From their position, they could just see through the ill-fitting blackout curtain. But they were still too far away to get a decent view. Erik propped his bike against a small tree and he and Magnus shuffled nearer, bent low until they were crouched directly below the window.

The music was even louder now. The boys hadn't really

heard much jazz before, certainly not for several years. Before the Nazis came, the village hall had regular dances and one of the locals had managed to get hold of a record of the Funny Boys to play on the gramophone. Erik, too young to be allowed to join in, remembered watching through the window as they danced. But no one had felt like dancing for a while now. And the village hall had been taken over by the Germans anyway.

The air was filled with the steady pluck of a double bass and some sort of woodwind instrument soared around piano chords. It all sounded so disjointed, yet strangely, a melody seemed to emerge and the beat was intoxicating. Before they knew it, the boys were bobbing their heads along, tapping their feet and grinning at each other. Erik snapped his fingers and swayed in time to the music. Magnus grabbed his hand urgently and signalled for him to be still. But Erik had no intention of sitting quietly. He pulled Magnus's hands and firmly shaped them into a step for his foot—the window was at some height off the ground and he needed a bit of help up. Magnus shook his head but Erik pleaded with a smile. 'Come on,' he seemed to mouth. Erik stepped into Magnus's cupped hands and, with his fingers on the ledge, he pulled himself up carefully so he could peek into the room.

Erik was pushing his luck with Magnus's patience. Erik, was the more adventurous of the two and he would often lead Magnus into situations that were a little daring. He didn't do it to be unkind; he was just more spirited. But

Magnus was always worrying—especially where the enemy was concerned. He would recount rumours he'd heard about Nazis: that they sent Jewish people away to work in labour camps and that Norwegian children with blonde hair and blue eyes had been rounded up and shipped off to Germany, never to be seen again. Some said many had died or had been murdered. Magnus often seemed overwhelmed with such fears, and he was no doubt concerned that his dad might find out they were 'Nazi-spying'. But although Erik could feel Magnus shaking with his weight, he edged his head up just a little further. Just a moment longer, he thought to himself.

It was a stark room, dimly lit. A shelf lined with books was visible on the opposite wall. A uniform hung on the back of the door. Extending his neck so he could lift his head up a little further, Erik could now make out a man lying back on a long chair. He wore thick patterned socks and had a shock of glossy black hair, but his face was hidden by the back of the chair. He was obviously smoking a cigarette as little puffs of smoke kept appearing directly above him. His toes twitched and wriggled in time to the beat. Erik stretched a little more to see his face. If only he could ease himself up just an inch higher, he'd be able to see over the back of the sofa. He pushed up on his toes. Magnus strained under the weight; he swayed a little, desperately trying to keep his balance. But he could hold on no longer and Erik's peeping came to a sudden end. Magnus stumbled, tipping Erik to the side into a large bush. Erik squealed loudly. With an awkward scraping sound, the music stopped abruptly. Erik pulled himself out of the bush and quickly pressed his back flat against the hut, breathing fast. They didn't see the face of the German pressed against the window above them, but they could sense it was there. Erik reached his hand down towards Magnus and whispered loudly,

'Run, Magnus! Run!'

The two boys bolted back towards the path. The only light was from the moon, with the dim glow from the huts now far behind them. They didn't look back. They ran, tripping and falling over stones and roots, until they made it back to the road. But they didn't stop there. They kept up their pace until they reached the village. They finally stopped and leant, doubled over, against the schoolhouse, heaving oxygen into their lungs.

'That was a close one!' laughed Erik breathlessly.

Magnus looked grim.

'You idiot!' he exploded. 'Are you trying to get us shot?'

But Erik wasn't listening. The smile had drained from his face.

'My bike!' he groaned. 'I've gone and left my bike outside the Germans' huts!'

CHAPTER EIGHT

The Chase

NORWAY 1944

Later that night, around midnight, Erik walked back to Magnus's house. The moon was bright and there was a soft stream of light coming from behind the shop door. Erik wondered if Magnus's father was waiting for someone: a Resistance agent perhaps. He moved quietly round the back of the house until he was directly under Magnus's room. He reached down and gathered a handful of gravel and threw it up towards the window. Erik waited. There was no response. He tried again. This time, a pale, disgruntled-looking Magnus appeared at the window. He opened it and leant out.

'I'm not coming, Erik,' he spoke in an angry whisper. 'I told you that earlier. Leave me alone. You're always pulling these kind of stunts.'

'Please, Magnus. You'll not get in any trouble, I promise!'

'You always say that, Erik. And we always get into trouble. It's your bike. You get it!'

'Hey! You wanted to see the Nazi ship didn't you?'

Magnus shut the window. A few seconds later he appeared at the back door. His hair was sticking up and he looked annoyed. He was still wearing his pyjamas, but with his black boots and a large overcoat on top.

'No funny business this time, right? We get the bike and get out of there.'

Erik nodded and they set off together, retracing their steps.

'That ship,' began Magnus.

'I know,' agreed Erik. 'I can't stop thinking about it.'

'They've tried to sink it. But—,' he paused and shrugged his shoulders.

'No one could sink that beast,' remarked Erik. 'It would take a million bombs.'

The road became a narrow track. They turned off and headed down the path that would eventually lead to the pebble shoreline.

'It was off to the left somewhere?' whispered Magnus, now aware that they must be getting nearer the radar huts.

'Yeah. A bit further down,' pointed Erik.

The gleam of the moon lit their way and in the distance the sea rippled and glittered softly.

'Here,' said Erik.

But just as they were about to turn, Magnus shot out a hand to stop Erik moving any further. In the still of the night, they could distinctly hear the sound of distant voices coming from the fjord.

'What's going on down there?' Magnus whispered.

Both boys looked towards the shoreline. A rowing boat cut smoothly through the still water, hugging the coastline. They crept further down the path, crouching so they would be hidden. They shuffled behind a large rock at a safe distance and peered over the top. They could hear voices chatting quietly to each other. Erik and Magnus froze. The voices weren't speaking Norwegian. They were German. The boat came closer. To move now would be too dangerous; they would be seen for sure. They stared at each other, eyes wide, and listened to the slice and pull of the oars getting steadily louder. Erik didn't dare look. He prayed the boat would continue further up the fjord, but there wasn't much further to go until they were into the open sea. He couldn't imagine they would want to be out there in such a flimsy vessel. What could they be up to he wondered? All that was left on this side of the fjord were the rocky cliffs— and caves. The boat was now almost opposite their hiding position. One German voice was quite demanding, angry-sounding. He must be the boss, Erik thought. He glanced over to Magnus who was biting his nails. But, to his relief, the boat didn't stop. The oars and the voices trailed away.

When it was safe, they came out from their hiding place and moved slowly back off the shore, heading towards the safety of the hillside. But Erik was too curious to leave it be. He knew a secret little pathway that wound its way along behind the rocks. They could stay low and observe what the Germans were up to. He signalled silently to Magnus to follow. But Magnus shook his head.

'Well, you stay here, then,' whispered Erik. 'I'll go.'

Magnus looked utterly horrified; Erik knew that he wouldn't want to be left alone. Through clenched teeth, Magnus nodded that he would follow Erik.

Erik led, deftly picking his way through the rocks; it was a treacherous path even in daylight. All the time they could hear the distant murmur of the voices and the steady rhythm of the oars slapping water. The boys occasionally stopped to listen: to check the boat was still moving. But now they heard splashing—the boat was being dragged up to shore. They crawled forward over slippery boulders until they could just see over the edge to the rocky caves below.

It was hard to make out exactly what the Germans were doing in the moonlight. There were three of them silhouetted against the water beyond; they seemed to be lifting large wooden crates or boxes out of the boat. Then they dragged them across the sand towards the cave. One man had a torch and lit their path. They must have taken the crates well inside the cave, as they disappeared for some time, their voices becoming muted. They came back for two more and again scrambled inside with their cargo.

From their vantage point above them, Magnus and Erik observed all the comings and goings. Magnus lay awkwardly; the top of his body was twisted in order to see as much as possible. He shuffled a little nudging Erik as he did so.

'What?' Erik breathed in Magnus's ear.

'Cramp!' came the reply through his gritted teeth. 'It's seizing up my leg!'

Magnus, clearly unable to bear it a second longer, kicked his leg to try to ease the pain. His boot hit a loose rock which flew over the edge and smashed into another rock below. Erik gasped. It was too late. Almost immediately, the torchlight revealed their position. There were shouts in German and, before they had time to think, the two boys bolted over the rocks. From their position, it would be impossible for the Germans to follow them up, but having finished their job, they leapt into their boat and started rowing furiously back along the shore line to catch the boys at the pebble beach. Panic gripped Erik. This was no schoolboy prank gone wrong; this was life or death. The Germans shouted as they ran, their torch scanning the rocks near them. They were watching their every move! The boys reached the pebble beach with seconds to spare. As they turned to run up the path, the boat landed and the three men leapt out and continued their pursuit.

What Erik did next was a mystery, even to himself. It was as if something pulled him to the German billets. An instinct perhaps? Or maybe he had simply assumed it would be the last place the Nazis would search. They turned down the track to the huts. Even in his panic, Erik noticed his bike was no longer propped against the tree where he had left it.

As they approached, they could see a man sitting on the steps, smoking a cigarette. Erik gasped, his heart pounding in his chest. They were surrounded; it was over. As they slowed down, the man stood up. In his mind, Erik pictured his family being interrogated. His father led away. Tears started to well up in his eyes. He looked to Magnus who had his head in his hands. The shouts of the Germans behind them were louder now. There was nowhere to run.

The man smoking the cigarette stood up quickly, his peace disturbed by this oncoming drama. He walked towards them, squinting into the dark. He quickly signalled for the boys to keep silent and to go into the hut. Erik and Magnus looked at one another, confused. They followed the instruction. After all, what choice did they have?

They dashed past the man and ran into the hut. Just inside the door there was a large cupboard against the back wall. Without saying a word, they scurried inside. Before long they heard raised voices—shouting—all in German.

Now footsteps were approaching the hut. Erik took a deep breath and braced himself. Magnus wept quietly. The footsteps stopped right outside the cupboard door.

Chapter Nine

The Werewolves

Lerwick, The Shetland Islands 2014

'This is crazy, Finn!' grumbled Gus, parking the van in the car park of the Bay View Care Home.

'We should be discussing this with Gran, not sneaking back in to see Olde. The "revenge" of what the hell was it? What did you call it?'

'The revenge of *Tirpitz*, and I'm telling you: this is properly weird,' explained Finn. 'These letters are, you know, pretty full-on. They're threatening. Like some say, "we know where you are, we know where your family is". I mean, does that mean us?'

'Which is why we should be talking to Gran. And the police,' he snapped, turning to stare at his brother. 'What exactly are we going to do about it, eh? We're hardly Sherlock and Dr. Watson, are we? We're just a couple of fishermen. And not particularly good ones at that—so dad tells us!'

'Yeah, but some of the letters say that any police involvement will be, you know, serious. That there'll be "repercussions".' Even Finn found it hard to believe. Was *any* of this realistic? 'He doesn't want anyone else to know, Gus, just you and me. We're not to tell dad either.'

Gus looked appalled. 'This is ridiculous nonsense, threatening some auld boy.'

They reached the steps to the care home and bounded up to the door. Finn felt a sense of relief. Relief that Gus was now involved. Gus was only a year and a bit older than him but he had a clear head and always knew what to do. Well, most of the time. He was confident though. That's why all the girls loved him.

Olde was in his room. He sat staring out of the window, twisting his fingers into knots. Music was playing on the radio, rather too loudly. Gus reached over to turn it down.

'Gus my boy!' he seemed to brighten. 'Finn's not been filling your head with my nonsense has he?'

'What's this about these letters, Olde? Can I see them?' Gus got straight to the point and pulled a chair closer to Olde. He was so much more relaxed with him.

Olde sighed and signalled to Finn to retrieve them out of the wardrobe. Gus leafed through the pile. There was a symbol at the bottom of each letter.

'What does this mean?' He held the thin paper up to the light. A large 'W' was imprinted on the fainter outline of a swastika. It was so faint it was almost a watermark.

'Nazis?' said Gus.

Olde nodded.

'I think so,' he sighed. 'Neo-Nazis,' he said with disgust in his voice. 'A group called "The Werewolves".'

'What do they want with you?' quizzed Finn.

'That's the million-dollar question, isn't it,' conceded Olde. 'It's a long story, boys. An old war time score to settle.' He reached to scratch his head.

'World War II,' said Gus; a fact rather than a question. He was obviously thinking out loud. 'What could you have done so long ago that even now the Nazis are after you? And what's *Tirpitz* got to do with it? What is this "*Tirpitz*" anyway? Some sort of ship?'

Finn stared at his great-grandfather who seemed lost in

thought; he was burdened with something. Something he maybe couldn't tell them.

Olde looked confused as if he didn't know where or how to begin.

'This really is a police matter,' said Gus, his voice tinged with authority.

'No,' said Olde firmly. 'You have no idea how powerful this group is. They're terrorists.'

'Even more reason to go the police,' said Gus.

'They've said clearly in several of the letters that going to the police will create serious repercussions,' said Olde. 'They will hurt my family. And they will hurt my old friend back in Norway whom they also seek to "punish".' He began knotting his fingers again.

'Boys. This group will *kill*,' Olde stated. 'It's me they want. They're avenging my involvement in something that happened in the war. Something I did. But there's another little problem they need my help with, before they finish me off.'

'What?' asked Gus.

Olde reached into the breast pocket of his shirt and retrieved another blue envelope, exactly like the others, only this one was bigger. He handed it to Gus who swiftly opened it and pulled out what appeared to be a newspaper cutting.

'This came the other day,' said Olde quietly. 'I've been mulling it over and so didn't keep it with the others.'

Gus unfolded the cutting to reveal a large, black newspaper headline:

Search for Tirpitz Gold Draws a Blank

He scanned the story below it.

'Gold? As in gold bars?' asked Gus.

'Yes,' agreed Olde. 'Nazi gold.'

Gus and Finn passed looks to one another. Olde sighed and

chewed his bottom lip. Then he took off his glasses so that his eyes vanished into his wrinkles and rubbed his index finger deep inside the crevices.

'The Nazis hid a lot of gold during WW2.'

'And what? You have it?' asked Gus, almost laughing. 'Hidden in here somewhere?' He smirked, looking round the tiny room.

'No,' said Olde, sharply, cutting through the humour. 'But that's just the thing. I did. I mean...,' he paused and searched the faces of the two boys. 'I know where there is rather a lot of Nazi gold. Or at least I *did* know. It was so long ago I...'

Finn and Gus stared at their great-grandfather.

'Somehow the Werewolves know that I know,' he added. 'And that is a mystery to me.'

'And they want you to show them where the gold is?' asked Finn.

Olde nodded and pointed a bony finger towards the envelope. Gus reached in and pulled out a small sheet of paper that had been tucked behind the newspaper cutting.

It's time this was returned to us.

Be prepared old man.

We're coming to get you.

Gus flipped the envelope over. The post date was two days ago. Their silence was abruptly interrupted by a sharp, urgent knock at the door.

CHAPTER TEN

Hans

NORWAY 1944

The cupboard door opened slowly. Ashen-faced, the boys crouched tensely awaiting their fate. Erik looked up and into the face of a smiling man with black glossy hair.

'Boo!' he chuckled softly. 'It's all okay boys. You can come out.' He spoke in clear Norwegian; his accent was so authentic, he could have passed for a local. Erik and Magnus stepped out into the hall of the hut looking around anxiously. Erik expected a fearsome looking Nazi to leap from the shadows with a gun. But the man in front of them smiled.

'They've gone,' he said to Erik and Magnus kindly. 'Now, how about a cup of hot milk? You've had…' he stopped, searching for the right words, '…a bit of a shock, I think.'

He ushered them into a small kitchen and set about warming a pan of milk on the stove. The boys nervously slipped onto the bench behind a wooden table. They looked at each other, not quite knowing what to do or say next.

'I have your bike, by the way,' said the German, placing two tin mugs of steaming milk on the table in front of them. 'I put it into the shed for safe keeping.'

'Thank you,' mumbled Erik.

He frowned at the two boys who looked suspiciously at their drinks.

'Boys, come on now. Drink up! I haven't laced your milk with poison!'

Erik smiled sheepishly and lifted the cup to his lips. It was warm and comforting; the milk tasted sweet and delicious. Magnus began to sip tentatively from his cup too.

'Where did the Nazis go?' Erik asked the German cautiously. 'I mean, why did you save us?'

The man rolled his eyes, 'Oh, they were idiots. Bullies. I told them I had no idea what they were on about and that no boys had come near the hut. I said they must have imagined such things at this time of night!'

Magnus's eyes widened. 'They saw us for sure,' he spoke for the first time. 'They shone their torch right at us.'

'What were you doing down there in the middle of the night, anyway?' asked the German.

The boys looked at each other and shifted uncomfortably.

'We came back to get the bike,' admitted Erik. 'But on the way down the hill we saw this boat coming up the fjord and followed it. We wanted to see what they were up to.'

The German stared at Erik. His eyes narrowed as he absorbed this information.

'Something they didn't want anyone to see,' he murmured, almost to himself.

Erik momentarily forgot he was speaking to the enemy and started to describe what they had just witnessed.

'The crates looked very heavy. They were hauling them into one of the caves,' he said. The German listened intently, frowning. Erik was about to continue when he bit his lip and stopped himself. The German laughed.

'Don't worry boy! I'll not run bleating to those...,' he paused and half muttered under his breath, 'idiots!'

Erik sank back relieved. But confusion seeped into his mind. Why was this man not supporting the actions of his compatriots? The German looked at his watch.

'All finished? You'll need to head off, boys. It's late, and you'll have school tomorrow, no?'

Magnus immediately slid off the bench, desperate to leave. Erik was in less of a hurry. Something didn't seem to fit; he felt unsettled.

Outside, the German casually lit another cigarette and sauntered over to the shed to haul out Erik's bike.

Magnus looked around him.

'They've gone,' the German said, the cigarette burning between his teeth. 'Don't worry.'

'Thanks,' said Erik awkwardly. He couldn't believe he was thanking a German. He felt his face flush. Lucky it was dark, he thought.

'My name's Hans,' the German added, holding out his hand. Erik hesitated but then he reached out and shook it. His grip was firm; it was reassuring.

'Erik,' he said. 'And he's Magnus,' Erik signalled to his friend with his upturned thumb. Magnus gave a nod but didn't shake his hand. Even in the dark, Erik was aware of Magnus glaring at him. Then they turned and started to head back along the path.

They didn't say much to each other on the journey home, but both boys knew they'd had a lucky escape. Erik guessed that Magnus would be quite prepared to leave it there and never talk about the incident ever again. But the next morning, on the way to school, he pushed to unravel the previous night's adventure.

'What d'you think those Nazis on the rowing boat were up to?' began Erik, wheeling his bike beside them.

Magnus yawned and rubbed his head, ruffling his tousled hair. His eyes were puffy.

'Dunno,' he said, 'Did you do that homework for Olsen yet?' he said.

'I couldn't get to sleep last night when we got back,' continued Erik, ignoring Magnus's attempt to alter his path of thinking. 'Those Nazis were hiding something pretty special. I mean, why else row out in the middle of the night?'

Magnus inspected his fingers carefully, then raised them to his lips and nibbled his nails.

'I think we should go back and have a look,' Erik suggested tentatively.

Magnus stopped and turned to Erik, his face now drained of colour.

'There is *no* way I am going back there,' he stated. 'Don't, Erik. Don't ask me to go with you!'

He stopped as a group of their classmates walked past them. Then he continued, his voice muted, his teeth gritted. 'We were nearly caught! Are you mad? How do we know they didn't see our faces? They could be coming here today to get us!' He was angry now. 'Or they'll guess that we're curious and be waiting for us down at the cave!'

Erik twisted his mouth to one side and eyed his friend carefully.

'Okay, okay,' he soothed. He would leave it a little while before having another shot at talking Magnus round. Maybe he could bribe him with the promise of some sweets? Or better still, chocolate, if he could get hold of some. That might do the trick! It wasn't that Erik hadn't appreciated the magnitude of what happened last night, it was just that he couldn't put it out of his mind. He had to find out the truth. He and Magnus had witnessed something that the Germans were desperate to keep a secret. That was worth holding on to and prodding a little further. Who knew what it might mean? It could be crucial: vital to the cause.

Erik left Magnus at the front of the school house and pushed his bike around the back.

'I've been waiting for you,' said a familiar, menacing voice. Out from the shadows, cracking his knuckles, stepped Kristoffer.

CHAPTER ELEVEN

Friends and Enemies

NORWAY 1944

Kristoffer grabbed Erik by the scruff of the neck and threw him roughly to the ground. His glasses fell onto the gravel.

'You little rat! You think you can hit me with a ruler and get away with it? I'll show you what we do to cowards like you!'

He lifted his boot and kicked Erik with a mighty thwack in the groin. Erik groaned as pain ripped through his body, his breakfast resurfacing rapidly up his gullet. He rolled over and threw up. Frothy foam languished on his lips and his eyes watered.

Kristoffer laughed.

'What's the matter, little rat?' He bent down and put his face to Erik's, his icy eyes boring into him. 'You crying for your mother?' Then with a grin, he lifted his boot once more for another kick, when a clear voice called out,

'Stop, boy!'

Kristoffer, still smiling, stopped and turned, clearly half expecting to see Olsen. But instead, he saw a tall man, wearing a uniform—a German with black, glossy hair. He spoke again in perfect Norwegian. It was Hans.

'Kick Erik one more time,' said Hans calmly, 'and I'll give you the beating your father should have given you years ago.'

Kristoffer placed his foot back on the ground and scowled.

'Get into school. Now,' snapped Hans.

Startled by this sudden display of authority, Kristoffer scuttled off. He threw Erik a backward glance, his lip curled.

Hans helped Erik up and looked around on the ground for his glasses.

'They're scratched, but not broken at least,' he said to Erik.

'Thanks,' said Erik, still shaking.

'Let's get you into class. Your teacher will be wondering where you are,' he said as they walked round to the front of the school. 'Are you okay Erik? He hurt you quite badly, I think?'

'I'm alright,' said Erik quietly. He paused then said, 'Why are you here? I mean, how did you know?' He was confused.

'I actually came to look for you. And Magnus said you were round the back,' said Hans.

'Came to look for me? Why?'

'Oh no! Don't worry! It's nothing bad. We need someone to help out a bit at the radar station. I wondered if you might want to do it?'

Erik looked doubtful.

'Helping you?' he asked, unable to hide his shock.

Hans smiled and nodded. 'We need someone to help with odd jobs around the station, you know, to make the coffee,' he joked. 'Or in my case, tea. We'll pay you a bit,' he cajoled him. 'Might come in handy for sweets! If you can get sweets these days.'

'I don't know,' said Erik. He was still a little shaken. 'How often?'

'Oh, not too much,' reassured Hans. 'Maybe an hour every day after school? Something like that?'

Erik sighed and bit his lip.

'Think about it,' said Hans. 'Come out and see us after school if you like.'

Erik nodded. 'Okay, I'll, I'll think about it,' he stammered.

'Excellent!' Hans beamed. He turned, still smiling, and walked down the street towards the village shop, whistling. It was the tune they'd heard him playing on his gramophone last night. Erik watched him for a second, then walked up the steps into the school house.

Kristoffer did not meet Erik's eyes for the rest of the day. In fact, he even picked up Erik's textbook when it dropped on the floor. It occurred to Erik that Kristoffer hadn't actually known who Hans was. He was so stupid, he would be worried that Hans was a German officer, with some senior Nazi connections. Erik wasn't about to put him right. The fact that Hans was merely a radar operator, and not a member of the SS, was something he would keep to himself.

Erik decided he wasn't going to say anything to Magnus about Hans's proposal, knowing he would disapprove. But it was Magnus who raised the subject after school.

'Well, what a strange day,' he said. 'Kristoffer comes into class, on time for once, looking pretty sheepish. And what did that German want? And why are your glasses all scratched?'

Erik didn't want to lie to his friend. But he also didn't want him to worry either.

'Oh, it was nothing. He just wanted to check we had got home okay and that we weren't too upset by what had happened.'

Magnus pulled a face of disbelief, 'What?'

Erik changed the subject.

'I think I might head up the coast road to Seal Point,' he said brightly. 'Catch a glimpse of an otter or two before dark,' he added quickly, to deflect from the fact that the German radar was positioned there. 'Or perhaps a sea eagle, if Kristoffer and his Nazi friends haven't shot them all on one of their hunting expeditions.'

Magnus frowned and shrugged his shoulders. 'I'll tag along too. Homework can wait!'

'Oh! Great!' lied Erik and, trying to ignore the ache from Kristoffer's kicking, pedalled the bike with Magnus perched on the back, this time towards Seal Point.

The road curved along the coast and when his legs became heavy with the uphill climb, Magnus hopped off and the boys walked pushing the bike alongside them. A gate stood at the end of the road and they clambered over it, leaving the bike behind. They trailed across the grass towards the rocky cliffs. From there, they could see the mouth of the fjord reaching the endless wild seas beyond. Seal Point marked the very tip of the fjord. Up to the right the great German radar stood, facing out to sea. The sun was now low in the sky and the boys sat down on the rocks. Erik fumbled in his satchel to find his binoculars and looked down around the shoreline for signs of otter movement.

'Not much doing,' he said distractedly.

'Here, let me,' said Magnus snatching the binoculars. He was now munching on a handful of cloudberries he'd found growing in a boggy clump nearby. Erik grabbed a few and tossed them absent-mindedly into his mouth. They were a little past their best perhaps, but still refreshing. He sucked on his lips, enjoying the juice as he looked up towards the radar station. He was curious.

'Let's go and see if Hans is around,' he suggested.

'What? No way!' said Magnus, startled. 'What? Is he your friend now? This German?'

'No!' said Erik, 'I just thought… after he helped us last night…'

'He's a *German*, Erik,' Magnus enunciated loudly. 'He's the enemy of Norway! They have taken over our country and you want to say "Hi"! Are you crazy?'

'Okay, okay!' soothed Erik. 'Something just doesn't add up about him. Why did he hide us last night? I think,' he paused, shaking his head, 'I think he's…'

'*On our side?*' asked Magnus. He stood up briskly and set off walking.

'Is that why you came up here?' he shouted back. 'To see your *friend* the German?'

Erik didn't say anything. It was useless trying to explain his hunch to Magnus.

'You're a fool, Erik! A fool,' Magnus yelled, some distance away now. 'I hope your father doesn't find out! Or mine.'

'Where are you going?' shouted Erik after him. 'You can't walk all the way back to the village.'

'Watch me!' snapped Magnus. 'I don't take rides from *quislings!*'

He walked off, back towards the gate. Erik sighed and shook his head. He stood up and wandered towards the radar station. As he approached, he hesitated. But something drove him on. He reached out his hand and firmly knocked on the door.

CHAPTER TWELVE

The Visit

LERWICK, THE SHETLAND ISLANDS 2014

Finn jumped. He stared anxiously at Gus and Olde. The silence was broken by Olde laughing.

'Come on boys! You don't think it's them do you?' he chuckled. 'Come in!' he called.

The handle turned and in marched a woman in lemon overalls.

'Good morning,' she began, then, clearly realising it wasn't just Olde in the room, added, 'gentlemen.' She brought in a tray of tea which she then proceeded to lay out on the small table. She seemed to sense she'd interrupted something tense.

'Everything alright?' she said, glancing around.

'Yes, yes, Heather,' said Olde in a cheery tone. 'These are my great-grandsons. They've popped in for an unexpected visit.'

'Aww,' remarked Heather with a smile. 'That's nice, boys.'

They smiled back mechanically. Finn tried to control the surge of adrenalin circulating through his veins. His breathing was quick and his heart was pounding. He looked over to Gus, who now folded his arms casually, but Finn noticed his jaw clicking.

'Must be your lucky week for unexpected visits,' added Heather. 'What with that gentleman calling in yesterday.'

Olde's face dropped. Gus and Finn stared at Heather.

'What gentleman?' Olde enquired, trying to sound calm.

'Oh,' said Heather. 'Did no-one tell you? That's terrible. I'll have a word with...'

'What gentleman, Heather?' urged Olde, anxiety creeping into his voice.

Heather paused, apparently gathering her thoughts.

'He arrived at the front desk—in the middle of the afternoon—I think, as you were having a nap. Very polite young man. Very tall. Broad. Blonde,' she listed. 'I'm so sorry. I thought someone had passed the message on.'

Olde and the boys leant forward in their seats and looked sideways at each other—hanging on her every word.

'And? Did he leave a name?' asked Olde, now trying to sound laid back.

'No, he said you would know who he was. He didn't want to cause any fuss,' she spoke carefully, as though trying to remember every detail. 'He said you were expecting a visit and that he'd pop back another time.'

'Oh yes,' lied Olde. 'I think I know who that was. I'm guessing, if it's who I think it is, that he didn't speak with a local accent?'

'No,' said Heather, in agreement, 'No he didn't, now you come to mention it. He sounded, well, a bit like you, dearie.'

'Norwegian?' added Gus.

'Well yes, something like that. Not from Shetland though. Such a nice young chap. Very smart. Very shiny shoes. You know, that's something I always notice in a man. Tells you something of his character,' her eyes trailed downwards.

Finn tucked his filthy trainers under his chair.

'Did he say *when* he might be back?' asked Gus. 'Sounds like a family friend of ours,' he added, 'always surprising us,' he rolled his eyes, trying to be light-hearted. Finn attempted to join in the humour with a nervous laugh.

'No, no, dearie,' he didn't. 'He just said he'd come back today at some point. And that he couldn't wait to have a good chat about the old days.' She seemed a bit puzzled at this, but she quickly snatched up the empty tray. 'Oh, and he said that you weren't to worry. He could always pop round to see your daughter Anna. It's nice when friends drop by unexpectedly isn't it?'

A look of horror spread across the faces of Olde and his great-grandsons.

'Right, my dears. I'll be back in later,' she smiled and bustled out.

As soon as the door was shut, Gus was up on his feet tapping into his mobile.

'Gran? Is everything okay?' His voice was tense as he pressed the phone to his ear.

Olde and Finn listened in to the conversation.

'Where are you?' continued Gus, clearly trying to make his voice sound as normal as possible. 'No, Gran everything's fine. I just heard there had been a car crash in the toon and wanted to check it wasn't you! You know how I worry,' he added. 'We'll see you later. By the way, has anyone called at the house today?' There was a pause. He shook his head at Olde and Gus; a look of relief flooded his face. 'No. Okay. That's fine. Nae probs. See you later.' He rang off.

'She's fine. She's round at a friend's for coffee,' he said, sounding momentarily reassured. He put his hands through his hair. 'Let's think this through,' he said, pacing the room.

'Think it through?' blurted Finn. 'We've got to get you out of here, Olde. Today. They're here! The Werewolves are here, in Lerwick! And they know where we all live! It's not safe. We have to call the police now. This is getting braaly serious,' he warned.

Olde paused. He too looked wide-eyed. 'And tell them what?' he added, almost mockingly. 'That we think some Nazi is after me? Think how ridiculous it all sounds. I don't think they're going to put that high up on their list of priorities, do you? And what do I do in the meantime? Wait here for another knock at the door?'

'So, we have to get you out of here.' stated Gus. 'But how do we do that without raising suspicion? I suppose we could just say we're taking you out for a wee walk—there's no law against that, is there?'

'It's a bit unusual. Could raise eyebrows,' said Olde, thinking as he spoke. 'And I'm always taken out in that blasted wheelchair. Which I don't really need,' he added.

Gus looked deep in thought.

'But it's not illegal,' he added. 'They can't *stop* us from taking you out somewhere for a bit?'

'Aye, but then what?' exclaimed Finn, his voice a little shrill now. 'We can't keep him in hiding in the toon forever. What are we going to *do* with him?'

Olde stared at Finn, and a scowl gathered his forehead into a tight knot of wrinkles. 'Him? *Him*? *What are we going to do with him*? That's no way to refer to *me*! I'm sitting here right beside you, Finn,' Olde growled.

'Sorry, Olde,' Finn stammered, 'I mean I dunno what we're supposed to do. You know you're not a young...' he stopped himself. 'I mean you're auld, Olde,' he added. 'You're not easy to... to, eh, move around. Or look after.'

Olde tightened his jaw and slowly closed his eyes.

They sat in silence. Finn searched Gus's face, hoping that his older brother was formulating a plan. Maybe they could lay low for a while until the drama had passed. Maybe the Werewolves would give up and slink back to wherever they had come from. Where *had* they come from? Finn had so many questions.

'Where's the boat at the moment?' asked Olde.

'It's in the harbour. Dad's away on holiday,' said Gus, now snapping out of his thoughts.

'You have the keys?' added Olde.

'For the boat, aye, they're hidden in the usual place in the wheelhouse. But why?' Gus sounded confused.

Finn glanced between them. Olde's motive dawned on Finn and he didn't like it. He pulled his hoodie up over his chin.

'Let's just go and take a wander down there,' said Olde. 'Tell them that you've made some changes to the boat that you'd like me to see.'

Gus and Finn exchanged worried looks. Finn didn't dare say anything now in case it came out wrong and he ended up offending Olde again. He managed a small shake of the head towards his brother. But Gus wasn't offering an alternative and there was a growing sense of urgency. What if the 'visitor' came back now? He could arrive at any time.

'I've not been down to the harbour for a while,' said Olde, wistfully.

'The boat's not been cleaned out properly since the last trip, Olde. It's no place to hang around, I can tell you that,' Finn said.

Olde stared at him then shrugged. 'Well, perhaps you're going to treat me to fish and chips, eh lads?'

'Okay,' agreed Gus cautiously. 'That sounds plausible. And the boat's a braaly good place to hide out for a bit. Until we think through what to do next.'

Finn sighed and rubbed the back of his neck. He was beginning to see it was the only option. They could always come back, if they had a change of heart.

'Right, pass me your rucksack, Finn,' the old man snapped with a spirited gleam in his eyes.

Finn hesitantly held out his bag. Olde snatched it up and quickly gathered up his belongings, stuffing them into the bag. His great-grandfather clearly had no intention of coming back tonight.

Olde had a plan.

Chapter Thirteen

Union Jack

Norway 1944

Magnus didn't make eye contact with Erik at school. And he didn't wait for him at the end of the day. Erik pedalled his bike along the road, deep in thought, on his way to Seal Point.

He had been working for Hans and his colleagues at the radar station for two weeks now. There were several German operators there, all working in shifts. Erik enjoyed it. It made life a little more interesting and, if he was honest, a little more exciting. All the operators spoke good Norwegian— especially Hans—and Erik had even learned a thing or two about how the radar worked. He didn't tell anyone what he was up to. Only Magnus knew, and although he was angry, Erik was certain he wouldn't betray his best friend.

Erik's main job was to make coffee, sometimes having to pedal over to their accommodation huts to collect milk and if they were lucky the odd slab of cake. Hans showed him how to make his tea—with a teapot. The other Germans laughed at this ritual. He got his precious tea from the enemy, they mocked. It was strange, but sometimes Erik forgot that *they were* the enemy. They were likeable and funny, particularly Hans. Sometimes, Hans would walk with Erik back to the accommodation while smoking a cigarette. He would put his gramophone record on and shout to Erik over the music, 'Benny Goodman, Erik!' The King of Swing!' They would smile and tap their feet along to the rhythm.

Erik was approaching the gate that led to Seal Point when something made him stop in his tracks. A large, black car was parked across the end of the road. A small Nazi swastika flag poked out of the front of the bonnet. It flapped gently in the breeze. The hub caps were silver and polished like mirrors. Erik propped his bike against the fence and looked towards the radar station. In the distance, he could see three men were walking quickly towards him. They were unmistakably German soldiers in trench coats and boots. Erik felt his heartbeat quicken. These were not ordinary German soldiers: this was the Gestapo. He waited. To go towards the station right now might be a mistake. So instead, he whipped out his binoculars and made to head down to the Point as if he were on one of his otter outings.The men paid no notice to him and marched up to the gate. From his position, Erik could observe them with his binoculars. They were now clambering into the car with stern expressions on their faces. Then the engine rumbled loudly and they drove away. Horror washed over Erik. It was a stark reminder. The radar station with its laughter and coffee belonged to the enemy. He felt consumed with guilt. Magnus was right. He was a fool; he felt ashamed.

He was heading back up to the gate when he heard a voice.

'Erik!'

It was Hans. 'Where are you going? Come back!'

Erik turned and walked back down towards the station.

'I don't think I should be doing this anymore. I'm a Norwegian, Hans! My family…' he hesitated. He shook his head. 'I'm sorry.'

'I understand, Erik. This war is a terrible thing.'

Erik nodded.

'But I want to show you something before you go,' continued Hans.

Erik shrugged and followed Hans into the hut. Everything was in its place. Through in the control room several of Hans's colleagues sat in position, their headphones on, at machines with blips and glowing lights. One man even turned to Erik and gave him a friendly wave and a wink. Erik reluctantly lifted his hand to wave back. Hans shut the door into the control room and faced Erik.

'I shouldn't be here,' mumbled Erik.

'Could you pass me my cigarette case, Erik,' said Hans.

Erik stared at him. Hans pointed to a shelf behind him on the far wall, where his cigarette case lay. He reached over, picked it up and stepped forward to give it to Hans.

'Would you mind opening it for me?' said Hans casually.

Erik frowned. What was this all about? But he clicked open the slim, silver case. He lifted the lid and looked at the neat row of pearly white tubes sitting snugly side by side.

'And if you could take out a cigarette for me?'

Confused, Erik reached into the tin and using the tip of his nail he carefully lifted out one stick. He passed it over to Hans, who deftly popped it into his mouth and reached into his pocket for matches. He lit the tip and a puff of smoke wafted between them. Erik loved the smell of the tobacco.

'And another. For later?' Hans said.

Erik began to feel annoyed. This all seemed ridiculous. He sighed and once again reached into the tin. But this time, his nail caught on something underneath. He looked down and saw a flash of red and blue nestled under the cigarettes. As he pulled out the second cigarette, with it came a piece of cloth. He glanced up at Hans who was now leaning casually against the door behind him, a half smile on his lips. He nodded, as if encouraging Erik to continue.

Erik passed Hans the second cigarette, which he tucked behind his ear. Then Erik held the cloth up in his right hand. It unfolded to reveal an oblong of silk. The pattern was instantly recognisable. It was a flag: it was a Union Jack. Now it all made sense.

CHAPTER FOURTEEN

The Resistance

NORWAY 1944

Erik woke with a start. Gravel rattled against his window pane. He leapt out of bed and looked outside. Magnus's anxious face stared up at him out of the dark. Erik gave him a wave then pulled on his trousers and threw on his thickest jumper. Once downstairs, he pushed his feet into his boots. He cautiously opened the back door and saw Magnus sitting on the porch steps. He jumped up the minute the door creaked open.

'You have to help!' he whispered. Even in the dark, Erik could see his eyes were swollen from crying.

'What's wrong?' he asked, moving Magnus well away from the house towards the trees at the foot of his garden.

'The Nazis came to our house about an hour ago,' he said quickly, his voice rising in panic. 'They took away my father. They've taken him for questioning.'

Erik listened intently, processing the information, piecing together the events. The previous morning something incredible had happened: the thunderous sound of bombing had echoed around the fjord. It hadn't lasted long—minutes perhaps—but it was a sign. An exciting sign. Something was afoot. Rumours were rife in the village that British bombers had targeted *Tirpitz*. She'd survived, they'd said, only because low lying cloud had blocked the bombers' view. But her days were numbered. On the next clear day, they said, *Tirpitz* would be finished. The Nazis were agitated. And, like cornered rats, they were at their most dangerous. Everyone was under suspicion.

'They know!' said Magnus, a large tear rolling down his face, his hand shaking as he wiped it away.

'What do you think they know?' pushed Erik.

'They said that illegal radio transmissions have been picked up from this area,' began Magnus, trying to control his panic. 'They said they know the Resistance is active around here, that the British know the location of *Tirpitz*. They're searching the house right now. They're looking for the radio. My mother is out of her mind with worry. They ordered my dad to dress and they marched him away. I think they've taken him to the village hall.'

'Will they find anything? Or anyone, at your house?' asked Erik. After all, several Resistance agents had been hidden there.

'There's no one hiding with us right now,' Magnus said, with some relief in his whisper. 'But my father has hidden a radio in the past for agents, I think. I don't know. He doesn't tell me anything. It's just what I overhear. Erik, what shall I do?'

Erik stared into his friend's eyes. There was only one thing he could suggest.

'Hans!' said Erik.

'No Erik. He's one of them! We can't trust him!' Magnus said desperately.

Erik grabbed him by the shoulders. 'He's our only hope. Don't worry. He's on our side. I promise.'

Magnus looked confused. He was in such a state of shock and so helpless, that he had no alternative but to go along with any plan that Erik suggested. Erik wheeled his bike out from the porch and grabbed his torch. He jumped on with Magnus behind him. They pedalled up the track and out towards the village. Once beyond it, Magnus shone the torch to light the road ahead of them. Erik propped the bike on a tree at the top of the coastal path and they began to swiftly, but carefully, weave their way down and along to the Germans' accommodation huts. They threw a handful of grit against Hans's window and waited. Finally, the curtain was swept to one side. Hans peered out, and as soon as he spotted the boys he pulled on his dressing gown and opened the door.

'What's the matter?' he asked.

'Tell him, Magnus. Go on,' urged Erik.

Magnus explained again what had happened that night while Hans listened carefully. Then, when he had finished, Hans spoke quietly and calmly.

'You've told me all I need to know. Go home now. And whatever happens, don't let anyone see you. Nobody must know that you've been here.'

Magnus looked desperate. 'But my father! What will

they do to him?'

Hans repeated his instruction. 'Go now, please.'

Erik frowned. He'd never seen Hans like this before: so serious and stern. He ushered them out of the hut and signalled for them to go. They made their way back up to the bike and Erik started to pedal towards the village. Not a word was spoken or whispered on their return journey; even in the silence that hung between them, Erik could sense Magnus's misery and despair. Erik wanted to reassure him, but he was fighting doubt. Suddenly, he felt a hand grasp his shoulder.

'I can hear something!' gasped Magnus close to his ear.

Erik stopped the bike. In the distance they could hear the quiet murmur of a car engine. Sound travelled in the fjord, particularly when there wasn't a breath of wind.

'A car!' whispered Magnus. 'And it's coming this way!'

Sure enough, they could make out the faint glow of shielded headlights beaming through the distant trees.

'What do we do?' asked Erik.

They couldn't go back. They couldn't go forward. One side of the road was a steep drop and the other was a sheer face of rocks. But if they stayed anywhere on this road, they would definitely be seen.

Quick as a flash, Erik leapt off the bike and threw it into a long, shallow ditch beside the road. They grabbed branches and sticks attempting to cover the bike, but all the while the engine was getting closer.

'You lie down, Magnus, I'll cover you too!' said Erik.

'What about you?' gasped Magnus.

'Just do it, Magnus!' snapped Erik.

Magnus lay in the ditch as flat as he could, and Erik speedily covered him with anything he could get his hands on nearby. Soon Magnus had a layer of grass, moss and twigs over him. The sound of the engine was now roaring towards them.

'Get down, Erik!' shouted Magnus.

Erik tried to bury himself beside Magnus—his face pressed into the dirt. He grabbed handfuls of moss and feebly attempted to throw them over himself. It was no use. He sat up and looked around, his mind racing. All the time, the engine's roar was getting louder and louder. And then, squinting through the darkness, Erik could just make out the carcass of a dead sheep lying a little further along the side of the road. There was nothing for it. He raced over and grabbed the beast by the legs. It must have been dead for some time. Its flesh was pecked and mauled until it was almost an empty carcass; its rotten stench instantly filled his nose, making him cough and retch. He hauled it over to the ditch and lay down, pulling what was left of its body awkwardly over his. As he did this, shielded headlights lit the road around him and the familiar rumble of an engine came sweeping round the corner. Erik gripped his eyes tight and waited.

It must have been that Nazi car he'd seen earlier: it was the Gestapo.

Chapter Fifteen

The Great Escape Part 1

Lerwick, The Shetland Islands 2014

'Remember to act normal!' whispered Olde to Gus and Finn. Finn bit his lip. This would be interesting, he thought, sweat bristling on the back of his neck; he was rubbish at lying.

They opened the door of his room and, flanked by his two great-grandsons arm-in-arm, Olde led them down the narrow corridor of the care home towards the front entrance. Olde wore his hat and coat. Finn lugged the rucksack, which was now stuffed full of Olde's belongings, on his back—it was surprisingly heavy.

'We're just off out for a wee jaunt,' said Olde brightly, to the woman sipping a can of juice at the front desk. 'Isn't that right, boys?'

'Right,' they said in unison. Finn rolled his eyes.

The woman was absorbed in something on her phone and had surreptitiously placed an earphone in one ear. She tore her eyes away from the screen for a matter of seconds to register Olde, and reached out to press the door release button, giving them the briefest of glances.

Too easy, thought Finn. Far too easy. He threw Gus a panicked look.

'You escaping somewhere?' shouted a voice from down the corridor. It was Heather, the care assistant, bustling along with a pile of fresh towels. She was smiling but even so, her gaze was steady; she was interested.

Damn, thought Finn. Nothing gets past her. Finn gulped and looked down at his feet, his face flushing. He could feel it spreading—his ears were beginning to burn.

'Yes! Heather!' said Olde smoothly. 'A bit of fresh air is in order. We might pop down to the harbour. Take a look at the boys' fishing boat, grab some fish and chips.'

'Oh?' said Heather, registering some level of surprise. 'That's nice. Not taking the wheelchair?' she added, a smile fixed on her face. But then her expression changed. Finn felt another surge of panic. 'But boys, it's blowing a hoolie out there!' She pointed towards the window.

They quickly looked outside. They hadn't noticed the change in the weather: the rain was horizontal. Finn pressed his eyes shut.

'What was that? What did she say?' Olde said loudly. He looked blankly at Gus and Finn.

Finn stared at him with a look of confusion and then turned to Gus. They shared an unspoken incomprehension at their great-grandfather's strange outburst. Why was he shouting? Why was his hearing a problem all of a sudden? He'd been fine five minutes ago.

Finn looked the other way; it was all getting too much. He stared out of the window. A car pulled up in the car park and a man got out. Even through the rain, Finn could make out that he was very tall and was wearing a dark jacket. He was broad, striking, with blonde hair and a confident air, even as he battled the elements. There was something about him that seemed a little out of place. Finn felt a growing sense of unease.

'It's raining, Olde,' Gus said irritably.

Finn nudged Gus to look outside at the man who was now moving at a brisk pace across the car park. Gus's eyes widened. It was him, it had to be him! Finn could see the Adam's apple in his brother's throat shift as he swallowed hard.

Olde looked blank. He shook his head as if he still didn't understand, as if there was soap in his ears. 'It's what?' he said again. His voice now ridiculously loud.

Horror gripped both boys. Finn and Gus watched helplessly as the man came ever closer.

'Raining!' shouted Heather, gesticulating to the window and the wild weather beyond. 'Urgh! Those hearing aids!' she said, exasperation in her voice.

'Olde!' hissed Gus, trying to casually draw his attention to the man outside.

'They must need new batteries,' continued Heather loudly, unaware of the drama unfolding. 'I'll pop and fetch them now!' she said. 'Since you can't possibly go out in that weather.' She turned and hurried off.

Olde wasted no time. As soon as Heather was out of sight, he lunged towards the front desk.

'We're in a bit of a rush dear, if you don't mind,' urged Olde to the woman, still fiddling with her phone. 'Tell Heather I'll see her later.'

She smiled absent-mindedly, still with her earphone in and dutifully pressed the door release button, returning her full attention to her screen.

The door lock clicked with a buzz just as the blonde man approached. Finn felt as though he was wearing lead boots and his legs were shaking, but Olde pulled him and Gus forward with surprising strength. Gus pushed on the glass, but as it shifted, he looked up and they all realised it was the man on the other side who was opening the door for them. Before they had time to react, a violent gust of wind whipped the door open, causing the man to stagger to catch it. And with the wind came a lashing of rain, right into their faces. Everyone grimaced—their eyes low, faces screwed tight. Olde dipped his chin, burying his face into the collar of his jacket. They shuffled out awkwardly, without anyone really looking each other in the eye. It was a lucky escape.

They didn't look back but moved as quickly as possible to the van. Finn threw off his bag, flung it in the back, and they all clambered in with Olde in the middle seat. Gus fumbled to get the key into the ignition. All the time they were all breathing heavily, checking the mirrors. Gus reversed with a screech and pulled out of the car park at speed.

'Well, if he wasn't sure it was me before, he'll know now!' said Olde.

'That was close!' remarked Gus quietly, pressing his foot on the accelerator. 'Any second now, the penny'll drop that he had you practically in his hand.'

'Just drive,' snapped Olde. 'Let's not give it a post mortem, eh Gus? I'm not sure my heart can take it!'

'How come you can hear alright now?' said Finn. 'You weren't hearing too well a minute ago!'

'A tactical diversion,' replied Olde, his hearing now miraculously back to normal. 'If in doubt, act as though you haven't a clue what's going on or being said. The very basics of sabotage. Heather will put it all down to dithery behaviour on my part. We now have a little time on our side.'

'Eh, not much time,' said Gus, glancing in the mirror.

Gus clearly didn't know where to go, or what to do. He was taking them up and down the sloping streets of Lerwick. Finn's mind raced too; somehow it didn't seem safe to go home. And if they did go home and the Nazi followed them there, then they were at a dead end.

Finn shifted in his seat, his jaw clicking nervously. Surely that guy would be on their tail any minute. But as they sped along the Esplanade, Finn knew Gus had made a decision, to go the harbour, to their fishing boat: *The Northern Light*.

'Where are you going Gus? Not the boat?' he said quickly, his nerves surfacing.

Gus didn't answer. He focused on the road. The van swung

into the car park, and Gus manoeuvred it to a spot hidden behind a huge lorry.

'It's the only logical place to go,' said Gus quietly.

Finn didn't argue.

They bundled themselves out of the van, Finn remembering to grab the rucksack. They couldn't move fast, what with the wind and Olde's weak legs, but nevertheless there was something of a determination in him. He gripped the boys' arms tightly and pushed on with force, despite the rain lashing in their faces.

The rain now mingled with the salty waves that crashed along the line of fishing boats jostling and rocking beside the wall. No one seemed to be around. All seemed strangely deserted in the screeching of the storm.

There was no time for discussion. They became absorbed in the challenge of guiding Olde on board *The Northern Light*, the family prawner. They had to lift him awkwardly over the rail. But Olde was small and wiry, and lighter than anything they were used to hauling on and off the boat. Once over, he was back on his feet, unfazed and beginning to move down the deck. Finally huddled inside the cabin, with Olde safe, they could gather their thoughts as handfuls of rain were flung against the small window.

'That was pure mental,' breathed Finn, wiping the rain off his face with his sleeve. His soaking hair clung to his head. 'What are we going do now, eh? Sail off into the sunset?'

There was a long pause. Olde rubbed his wrinkly chin with one hand and looked curiously at his two great-grandsons.

'There's no way back for me now, boys,' he said earnestly. 'The Werewolves are going to hound me to the end. To avenge the deaths of those on board *Tirpitz*. And to find the gold.'

'So here's an idea... Maybe don't tell them!' blurted Finn. He kept glancing back down the harbour wall.

'What? And have them torture me? Or my family in the

process?' replied Olde, calmly. 'No, I have to face up to this. Before anyone else comes to harm.'

'What do you mean anyone *else*?' asked Gus.

Olde sighed and pursed his shrivelled lips.

'They told me in one of the letters that they'd got my "accomplice",' said Olde. 'I don't know if they were bluffing but...'

'But what?' pushed Gus.

'The letter said that they had paid him a visit and that they had ways of making him "talk" and that if I called the police, or alerted anyone else, they would kill him.'

He paused and took off his glasses to rub his face. He looked up, his gloopy eyes glistening. 'Don't you see? *It's my fault they've got him!*' he said, his voice trembling, his face twisted. 'It's my fault he's involved. He was... good to me all those years ago.'

He shook his head, a look of desperation in his face. 'I know I'm just an old man. But...'

He stared at the two lads in front of him.

'I have to go there. To find him. I can't just pretend I know nothing about any of this. It's an old score. So let's settle it once and for all! Don't you see?'

Finn frowned. He couldn't really see. He couldn't get his mind around all this cryptic cloak and dagger stuff. They were talking about the sort of thing you might see in a film. An old black and white one at that. He put his head in his hands. What on earth could they do?

'But where?' said Gus. 'Where is this gold? Where is your friend—this "accomplice"?'

'Norway, of course!' said Olde. 'We have to sail to Norway!'

CHAPTER 16

Bike Ride

NORWAY 1944

Erik shifted uncomfortably under the weight of the decomposing sheep. He could feel something trickling down the back of his neck. His eyes stung and he felt sick. The car passed, but he lay quite still until its engine was a distant hum. He wriggled out awkwardly from under the beast; his hands and clothes now reeked of rotting sheep. Still crouched low, he cautiously glanced up and looked back down the road. Magnus raised his head from under the moss.

'Who was that at this time of night?' whispered Magnus.

'Nazis,' said Erik.

'Thank God they've gone,' said Magnus, jumping up and pulling tufts of moss from his hair.

'But for how long?' said Erik quietly. 'This road is a dead end. They'll be back. We need to hurry. We've got to get back to the village before they decide to return. We may not be so lucky a second time.'

The boys quickly rescued the bike from the ditch, pulling off branches and leaves. They clambered on and Erik cycled as fast as he could with Magnus grasping him tight around the waist. This time, they didn't use the torch and pedalled through the darkness, barely lit by the distant glow of a pale moon. They didn't talk; they were too busy listening for the drone of the car engine. Erik held his breath. Sometimes they thought they heard it and Magnus would swivel around to catch a glimpse of the headlights.

By the time they made it back, Erik was panting and sweating. There was nothing more they could do. Helplessly, they parted company by Magnus's house and Erik sped off homeward bound, hoping and praying that somehow Magnus's father would be safe.

Back at home, Erik dumped his clothes in the porch. The smell was so pungent the whole house would be smothered by it. He would have some explaining to do in the morning.

He didn't feel like going back to bed—he was too alert. Where had that Nazi car been going? Why was the Gestapo involved? Driving along that road in the middle of the night, that car undoubtedly had something to do with Magnus's dad. He quickly dressed again, pulling on a navy blue sweater, black trousers and his thickest socks. He set off into the silent, black village and, dumping his bike near the churchyard, took off his shoes and continued on foot.

Taking great care to remain unseen, he moved silently in his socks along the road towards the village hall. The Germans kept the hall for their own uses now. At points, Erik had to feel his way, the darkness was so dense. Every so often, the clouds would shift and the moon offered a soft gleam to the streets, outlining familiar buildings and landmarks.

As he approached the hall, he could make out the outline

of a German soldier standing guard outside the door. He tucked himself behind a stack of crates and waited. The windows that ran along the side of the building were blacked out, but Erik noticed there was a tiny pinprick of light radiating from one of the windows. Magnus's father must be in there now; would they have hurt him? Were they holding a gun to his head? He shuddered at the thought. There was no noise. The silence was as intense as the darkness. There was no sign of the Nazi car either. He would have to wait.

Erik heard the door of the village hall open and two voices muttering in German. Were there two of them now? Or had one gone back inside? A match was struck. Two cigarettes were lit; their orange lights danced in the night. Erik could hear each intake of breath and the lights glowed brighter. But then one seemed to move in his direction. Listening to the footsteps, he realised with horror that one of the soldiers was coming closer. Erik made himself as small as he could, pressing close to the crates. Had the soldier seen him or heard him breathing? Fear flooded his veins. But the footsteps stopped. The soldier stood quite still, listening. Now, they could all hear it—the familiar hum of a distant engine. Erik momentarily relaxed, relieved at this distraction.

One of the soldiers shouted to the other in German and the orange lights were instantly dropped and disappeared, ground flat beneath heavy black boots.

Erik took a deep breath. The growl of the engine grew louder. Within a few minutes the car had come to a standstill a few feet from where Erik was hiding. Even in the depths of darkness he could see the gleam of the polished hub caps and the flash of the shiny black car doors as they swung open. Every sound seemed amplified. Boots crunched on the rough gravel, car doors slammed—but he could see no faces. They must have brought someone back with them. But who were they fetching at this time of night? Voices spoke sharply in German as they moved towards the door of the village hall. Erik was frustrated. He couldn't stay there all night waiting and wondering. Perhaps there was nothing more for him to do. Poor Magnus, he thought; his father was in grave danger.

And then he heard it. One of the men began to whistle softy. The tune was familiar. It was the jazz he'd heard on the gramophone. It was Benny Goodman—"The King of Swing"!

The Nazi car had brought back Hans.

CHAPTER SEVENTEEN

Radar

NORWAY 1944

Magnus waited for Erik at their usual meeting point the next morning.

'What's happened with your father?' said Erik, as they wandered down to the school. 'I went to the village hall last night.'

'You did what?' gasped Magnus. 'Are you crazy? The Gestapo was everywhere!'

'I know, I know. I just stayed to see the car return,' explained Erik. 'I was sure it had something to do with your father and I wanted to find out. And it did. They brought Hans! But I don't know any more than that.'

'They released my father sometime last night,' said Magnus softly. 'Or rather, very early in the morning.'

Erik stared at him and breathed out a sigh of relief. But Magnus looked pale and drawn. Erik could see the strain and worry etched in his face. Magnus looked around to check they were completely alone.

'Those damn Nazis,' he spat the words under his breath. 'He's battered and bruised,' he continued quietly. 'He's not in a good way, Erik. They've threatened him with being sent away to a concentration camp, or with being shot if they discover any more information that links him with the Resistance.'

'But what did they bring Hans in for, I wonder?' asked Erik.

'Father said they brought in some German radar specialist to help them with their investigation,' explained Magnus. 'And that he told the Nazis they were wrong, and to release my father immediately.'

Erik pushed his bike along, deep in thought as he ran over the events of the previous night. So that was why Hans had been so abrupt with them. He must have guessed that the Gestapo would come to him for help when they couldn't find the radio—they needed to draw on his expertise.

Erik didn't reveal to Magnus the truth about Hans and his allegiance to the British and their allies. He wasn't sure that now was the right time. And perhaps he too had a flash of doubt in his mind.

After school, he pedalled back down the coast road towards Seal Point. He passed the dead sheep lying by the side of the road and remembered with disgust the stench that had filled his nostrils the previous night. His mother had been horrified to find his foul smelling clothes waiting in the porch. He'd concocted a story about how he had fallen off his bike into a stagnant rock pool where a sheep had met its death. Fortunately, she hadn't questioned him further but had thrown her hands up in horror. He hadn't waited to hear anymore and had run out the door before the lecture could continue or before she set him to work scrubbing the whole lot clean. If they weren't so poor, she would have thrown them in the fire.

He arrived at the gate, and as he propped his bike against the fence, he noticed Hans and several other men outside. They were standing beside the great radar structure that looked out to sea. But Erik could see that it now faced inland; it had been rotated. The men seemed to be checking its new position.

Erik was careful not to ask many questions as he joined them on their way back into the radar station.

'Shall I make the coffee?' he asked.

Hans seemed a little distracted.

'Yes, yes, that would be good, Erik,' he said, running his fingers through his thick hair.

'You've turned the radar I see?' Erik added, moving over to the small stove and reaching for the coffee pot.

'Ah yes!' laughed Hans. 'Very observant of you, Erik! We have to be extremely careful to track where the British bombers are coming from They like to keep us on our toes!' He said this almost a little too loudly, so that he was within earshot of his colleagues. 'Erik, I need to head back to my hut,' he added. 'I have some things there I need to collect before I start my next shift. Perhaps you would like to join me?'

Erik followed Hans outside and they walked together up towards the gate.

'Something has happened, Erik,' he said cautiously. 'We have almost been expecting it. There was an attack on *Tirpitz* yesterday morning.'

'Yes,' said Erik quietly. 'Everyone heard the bombs. 'But...'

'The bombers came across land, from Sweden,' continued

Hans. 'That's why we've turned the radar. You see, the allies know exactly where she is.'

'How do they know that?' asked Erik. He was testing him a little.

'The Resistance have told them, through radio communication,' explained Hans. 'There are agents working up and down the coast of Norway passing on information about where *Tirpitz* is located.'

'So that's why the Gestapo raided Magnus's home—and arrested his father? They think *he* radioed the allies?'

'Him or a Resistance agent,' said Hans. 'They've been watching Magnus's father. They strongly suspect he's involved with the Resistance. They've observed strange comings and goings at the Johansen's house and shop.'

'But they couldn't find the radio?' said Erik.

Hans shook his head. 'They searched every nook and cranny of the house, but they did not find a radio. But their direction-finding equipment told them otherwise.'

'Why did they bring you in?' asked Erik.

Hans looked at him surprised. 'How did you know? You saw me?'

'You sent us away last night so abruptly I had to know more,' said Erik.

Hans shook his head and curled his lips into a smile. 'You have the makings of a good spy, Erik!'

He reached into this pocket and pulled out his cigarette case. Hans flipped open the silver lid and popped a slim white stick into his mouth. He felt in his pocket again, this time for matches and, after he struck a match alight, cupped his hands over his mouth. The cigarette tip now glowed and a long trail of smoke slipped from his lips as he began to talk.

'There's not much I don't know about radios,' he said confidently. 'And radars. The Gestapo paid me a little visit the other day and they realised that I'm good at my job. Experts in such things are pretty rare up here in the Arctic Circle.'

'So they brought you in to help?' asked Erik.

'Yes. But I managed to persuade them they had made a mistake. Or rather, that their equipment was flawed. It wasn't difficult. Their knowledge of such things is next to nothing.'

Erik processed this information. 'So Magnus's dad was released because of you?'

Hans nodded.

'Does he know that?' asked Erik. 'That if it hadn't been for you, he might have been shot?'

'Yes, I think we have an understanding. Per Johansen knows me already,' he said quietly. 'I've been doing work for the Resistance for some time, helping them with radio communication.'

He turned and placed his hands on Erik's shoulders. 'But you need to warn him from me, Erik.' He looked serious. 'I can't go near him now. They'll be watching Per —and my every move. I told them that their equipment had picked up signals coming from the radar station. Not from an illegal radio. You need to let me know as soon as Per has moved the radio to a new location so that the Resistance can safely continue its work. So that we can *all* continue our work to bring this war to an end.'

'Of course,' said Erik. He had a million questions swimming around in his mind.

'Why are you doing this?' he blurted out the question he had been longing to ask, but didn't dare. 'You're a... a German.' As he said those words, he felt a strange sensation flood over him. One of guilt, betrayal, disloyalty. But to whom? The loyalty he felt to his own country, his own people, was so strong, so defining, that he was baffled as to why anyone else would turn on their own. But, of course, he did understand, really; the Nazis had divided their own people.

A flicker of humour passed over Hans's features. He shook his head and sighed. Then his face fell to a grim look of distaste. 'What my people have become, because of... *him*...' He trailed off, lost in thought. 'The *Führer*,' he muttered. He took another drag on his cigarette, as if to snap him back to the present.

'Erik, I am going to need you to help now, in transferring messages for me to Per,' said Hans earnestly. 'I can't meet him in person. It's too dangerous. Nor can I write messages down in case they are found or intercepted.'

'Of course,' said Erik slowly. 'But what can you really do?' Defeat somehow seemed inevitable. 'What can any of us really do to end this war? It's too big for us!'

'Small steps, Erik. Have faith. Small steps can lead to great and powerful victories. You will see. This next stage is crucial. I need you Erik. It won't be for long. Perhaps another week or two. And then I'll be gone and you'll be out of danger.'

'Gone?' exclaimed Erik. A shiver rippled down his

spine. 'What are you planning, Hans?'

'*Tirpitz*,' he said quietly. 'Now it's time to finish her, once and for all.'

CHAPTER EIGHTEEN

The Great Escape Part 2
LERWICK, THE SHETLAND ISLANDS 2014

Gus frowned. 'But whereabouts in Norway, Olde?'

Norway wasn't particularly an issue. The boat sailed halfway across the sea to Norway most weeks.

'Ah!' said Olde. 'Well, that's the tricky part, I'm afraid,' he added cautiously. 'It's not an easy journey, or an easy place to get to. We have to sail almost to Tromsø.'

'Tromsø?' Gus said, as if he wasn't sure where that was.

'Above the Arctic Circle?' asked Finn. 'Are you crazy? In this boat?'

Gus looked shocked that his brother knew where Tromsø was.

'Is it fuelled up?' asked Olde.

Gus nodded.

Finn felt a steady pounding now going on inside his head. He pressed his hot temples on the glass of the wheelhouse. The storm was passing and the dark clouds were softening as the sun broke through once more. Gus too seemed deep in thought and leant his head on the glass beside his brother. Suddenly, he jerked his body back abruptly away from the window. His ashen face turned to Olde and Finn.

'The Nazi!' he whispered. 'He's here!'

Immediately, he squatted down, even though they were still well out of sight. 'I can see him in the car park,' Gus gasped through his teeth.

Finn slithered to the floor to join him and Olde wriggled his body down in the seat.

'How the hell did he find us here? He couldn't have followed the car, could he? There wasn't time!' Finn said horrified, his heart thumping.

'He'll know a lot more about us than you realise,' warned Olde. 'Finn, reach over to your rucksack, would you. Look inside, at the very bottom, wrapped in some clothes.'

Finn scrabbled along the floor and grabbed the rucksack. He fumbled with the zip and pushed his hand inside, rummaging to reach the bottom.

'How far away is he?' asked Olde.

Gus carefully inched his head up to the window to look out.

'He's a bit away. Seems to be looking for us—but maybe he doesn't know which boat we're in. He's checking out the first boat—I dunno, is he working his way down?'

'Gus, go and untie the boat,' said Olde calmly.

Gus and Finn both swung their heads round.

'What? Go out there now?' said Finn. 'Don't Gus, it's not safe!'

'Do it,' said Olde. 'Put one of the oilskins on and do it. Be casual about it.'

Gus nodded. On all fours, Gus shuffled over to the door and reaching up grabbed a yellow oilskin from the hook on the wall. He swung it round his shoulders and slipped his arms through.

'Where's the key, Finn?' asked Olde. 'But don't start the engine until Gus gives the signal. Get it ready in the ignition.'

Gus pointed to a small ledge under the dashboard. Finn dropped the bag and fumbled around for the key.

'Go,' croaked Olde, stretching up his head.

Gus slipped out the door.

'Well, Finn,' growled Olde. 'Where's the damn key?'

His fingers stretched and felt for the key. But instead, he

nudged it from its nook; it fell and slid across the floor into a deep crack.

'Oh for God's sake!' he muttered, his shaking fingers trying to poke it out.

'Hurry up!' snapped Olde. 'Gus'll be back any second!'

All of a sudden, Gus burst back in.

'We're loose. C'mon Finn, start the engine!'

Panic engulfed Finn as he crouched on the wheelhouse floor.

'What are we doing?' wailed Finn. 'We can't sail that far in this boat. We'll never make it. And dad'll kill us! This is pure mental Gus—mental!'

'Awww crap!' snapped Gus, his head in his hands. His face was flushed. 'Finn's right, Olde, we can't do this. It's crazy,' he said, almost pleading. 'Look, we can call the police. They'll sort it out. The guy out there, I mean, really. What's he going to do to us?'

Suddenly, they were interrupted. 'Hey! I know you're in there,' shouted a voice outside, with a thick Scandinavian accent. 'I only want to have a little chat.'

Gus, Finn and Olde froze. The man stood on the harbour beside the boat. Hidden by the side of the cabin, and glancing out the corner of his eye, Gus pressed his back to the wall.

'Come on now, boys, don't make me come aboard,' the voice continued mockingly.

Gus inched his head up, just high enough to peer out.

'What's he doing?' he mumbled, almost to himself. 'He's got something in his jacket...' Then his tone changed, 'A gun,' he whispered, urgently. 'He's got a gun!' He slid back down.

There was an intense pause.

'Well, boys,' asked Olde. 'Are you in?'

Finn didn't wait to be told again. Instinct seem to take over and a surge of defiance. He gouged his finger into the crack, retrieved the key, and reaching up slotted it into the ignition, flicking it hard to the right. The engine fired up.

'Hey!' yelled the voice outside.

The man outside grabbed onto the railing with one hand. The other still clutched the gun inside his jacket.

'What's he going to do now?' Gus said, looking out. 'Vault over into the boat?'

Now up on his feet, but crouching low, Finn steered the boat, straining to see out of the windows as he did so. The boat instantly began to move away from the harbour wall.

'Hey!' the voice shouted again, this time more urgently. The man gripped the rails with two hands, stalling the boat.

'What the hell?' yelled Finn. 'He's holding us!' The engine shuddered and strained but the gap between the man and the boat widened.

'Keep it going Finn, keep it going,' said Gus steadily eyeing the distance growing between the boat and the harbour wall.

The man had no time to jump now. If he continued to grip he would fall into the water. Finally, he let go and staggered backwards, his face twisted with anger.

'Where do you think you're going?' he shouted angrily as the boat picked up speed. He started to follow on foot along the harbour, staring at Gus who was now visible through the window.

'We'll find you wherever you go!' he warned. But as the boat pulled out into the wide expanse of water, they were safe. For now.

Finn, Olde and Gus looked back. The figure remained on the harbour. Frozen. Watching.

Finn continued to steer, glancing behind them from time to time. They were all quiet. The rhythm of the engine was the only sound.

'Well done, boys,' said Olde as Gus helped him shuffle into a sitting position. The rucksack Finn had been raking through tipped onto its side and a piece of clothing tumbled out with a thud. There was something hidden inside it. Something that now lay gleaming on the floor. It was a gun.

Olde raised an eyebrow, Finn's mouth dropped open.

Finally, Finn broke the silence.

'So,' he said, almost brightly, turning back to the steering wheel. 'Tromsø then?'

Gus nodded, gulping hard.

Olde stared out to sea, a trace of a smile on his lips. There was no way back. There was nowhere to hide.

CHAPTER NINETEEN

The Secret Room

NORWAY 1944

Crouched together in Magnus's attic, Erik slowly and carefully passed on the message from Hans to Per Johansen. The musty room was cramped and crammed full of boxes—stock for the shop below. There was muffled chatter from downstairs, and the ring of the bell on the shop door as customers came and went, gathering their supplies from Magnus's mother, who was looking after things. Through the skylight came the persistent cry of a seagull.

Magnus's father listened intently while he absent-mindedly sorted various tins and jars. He frowned, deep crevices appearing etched into his rugged face as he pushed his cap back and scratched his head. Then he nodded slowly.

'This is dangerous work, Erik,' he said quietly, placing the tins from his hands into a box on the floor. 'But vital.'

'Can we really trust this German?' said Magnus. 'How do we truly know that he is on our side?'

'He's proved his credentials,' interjected Per. 'He is well known to the Resistance agents. He's been working against his own people for many months. It was Hans who smuggled the radio here in the first place—passed on from an agent who came from Shetland. It was hidden inside a suitcase under a gramophone player, of all things! Don't ask me how he did it. But I trust him.'

Magnus nibbled his finger nails, his face a little sulky.

'And Hans skilfully cast doubt on the accusations against me regarding the radio,' explained Per. 'The Gestapo didn't like it. And in doing so he put himself at risk. They will be watching him too now. We are all being watched. Such is the ripple of suspicion.'

'Just tell us what you want us to do, father,' Magnus said.

Per turned back to his tins and jars and continued sorting.

'We need to find somewhere,' he said. 'Somewhere hidden, where we can use the radio safely,' he said. 'It sounds so simple, does it not, boys?' He reached over and placed his hand firmly on one section of the wooden panels that enclosed the attic space. And then, with a violent push, there was a scraping of wood and the panel shifted forward. With one further shove, it fell flat with a thump. A cloud of dust rose into the stale air. Erik and Magnus gasped. Hidden in the eaves of the house was a secret room. This was where the radio had been hidden! Two chairs sat either side of radio equipment. A tin mug lay on the floor along with some paper and a couple of pencils.

Erik shuffled through into the room to take a closer look. He didn't dare touch the radio, as if it were somehow contaminated and the Nazis would smell it on him the moment he wandered out onto the street. It sat innocently tucked inside an old, battered leather suitcase. There was a tangle of wires growing out of it and it seemed to Erik as if its surface was a mass of dials and switches. And yet, this simple box could help them beat the Nazis.

'With this radio, my agents can confirm that *Tirpitz* is still in her location at the top of the fjord at Tromsø,' Per explained. 'Then we can receive intelligence about the next allied planned attack. We can't operate the radio here as the Nazis will know; we have to take it somewhere else. But where?'

Erik sat in silence, his mind racing. Then he began to nod. The nodding became more and more excited.

'Of course!' he gasped. 'The mountain caves!'

A smile grew on Magnus's face. 'Great idea, Erik!' Then he looked to his father who maintained his craggy frown.

'Father?' he said, shrugging his shoulders. 'Well? What do you think?'

Per nodded. 'Yes,' he conceded. 'It could work. But how are we going to smuggle that,' he said pointing to the cumbersome radio equipment, 'up a mountain? Nazi soldiers are outside the shop! Not to mention Gestapo swarming all over the village hall.'

'So we need to hide the radio in something. Something that the Nazis wouldn't think to investigate too closely,' added Magnus.

'Or something they wouldn't want to investigate too closely,' added Erik smiling. Magnus and Per looked at him blankly.

'Stockfish!' he announced, grinning.

Per and Magnus listened closely as Erik outlined his plan. 'We pack the radio into a basket and we cover it carefully with something to protect it...'

'Like waxed cotton perhaps?' suggested Per.

'Yes,' agreed Erik. 'Then we cram some particularly smelly, rotten stockfish on top—there's some in an old boat shed of ours down by the water—the roof caved in a while ago and the fish stored in there is absolutely foul. You can almost smell it a mile away. Once the radio is all packed inside, we can borrow our old fjord horse and take it up to the mountains!'

'But why?' asked Magnus. 'The Nazis will wonder why on earth we're taking stinking old stockfish up to the mountains. They would be suspicious.'

'Not if we tell them that we're taking it up to the Sami in the mountains for their dogs,' he said. 'The dogs will love it. We can take up some good stockfish too.' Magnus continued to look confused. Erik explained, 'My family have had strong links with the Mountain Sami for generations and we often give them gifts. In return, they give us reindeer meat.'

Erik looked at Per and Magnus, warily waiting for a reaction. They said nothing.

'And right now they are gathering their reindeer together, ready to move. They'll be leaving soon so we have the perfect reason to be taking them a gift.'

There was a long pause. 'Don't you see?' urged Erik. 'It would be entirely normal for us to be going up there with the stockfish. Besides, the smell will be so bad that the Nazis won't want to come too close!'

Per let out a small chuckle. 'I think you may have a good plan there, young Erik,' he said. 'We'll make an agent out of you yet, boy!'

Magnus looked a little hurt. But Erik gave him a light punch on the shoulder. 'Shall we go and raid the old boat shed?' he laughed, clutching his nose.

Chapter Twenty

Stockfish

Norway 1944

Erik's horse was tethered outside the shop. Inside, tucked away at the back, Erik and Magnus prepared the baskets for the horse to carry up the steep mountainous pathway. The previous night, Erik had gathered a few batches of slimy, fetid fish from the old boathouse to store in Magnus's shed. They'd also taken some dry stockfish from another of Erik's father's storerooms and attached it so that it would hang from the side of the basket. The Nazis would recognise it immediately from its distinctive headless shape; stockfish was always looped over large racks along the coastline in the spring.

When they returned to the shed in the morning, the smell was unbearable. Choking and coughing, they packed the damp, pungent fish on top of the radio. It had been carefully packed in its suitcase and then wrapped in an old fishing jacket. In the other basket, also wrapped in a piece of waxed cotton found amongst fishing odds and ends, was the heavy battery.

The smell caught the back of the throat. Dried stockfish was bearable, but when it became wet and then began to ferment, the smell was putrid. Magnus and Erik buried their mouths and noses into their thick sweaters as they worked.

'I hope to God that this works,' said Magnus.

Erik laughed.

'Do you think the Nazis will come anywhere near us? They'll be staying as far away as possible!'

Carrying a handle each, the boys lumbered through the shop with the first basket. They tied it securely to the horse and, without looking up to see if they were being watched, they went back for the second and final basket. Per supervised from behind the counter. He had checked the baskets carefully himself to make sure the radio and battery were well hidden below several layers of fish. And now, with his hand over his nose, he held the door open for them as they staggered through for the last time and muttered a hurried goodbye. Nothing should raise suspicion that this was in some way an unusual or dangerous outing.

With the baskets safely secured, Magnus and Erik set off with Erik leading the horse along the village street, the large dried fish swinging from side to side. Erik tried to relax— to give the impression that this was the most normal thing in the world for them to be doing. But he shot Magnus a shifty look. There was a German officer stationed outside the shop. He must have seen them load up the horse, but now he was smoking a cigarette leaning casually against a wall. They continued on, passing a group of Germans who stood laughing and chatting together outside the village hall: the Gestapo headquarters. But nobody so much as glanced in their direction.

'Easy!' murmured Erik quietly. And he gave Magnus a wink. But just as he said this, he heard a shout.

'Oi! You boys! Stop!'

Erik's heart dropped to the ground. He froze, his heart thumping in his throat. He and Magnus looked first to one another and slowly turned around. A German soldier had broken away from the group and was walking purposefully towards them. He was holding something. What was he doing? Did he suspect? And then it dawned on Erik.

'Here, this dropped off your basket,' said the German, handing them a large pair of stockfish.

Erik sighed, then faked a laugh and stepped towards the German.

'Thanks!' he said grabbing the fish and reattaching it onto the basket.

'That's quite a load you've got there,' remarked the German.

'Yes, yes, it's a gift,' interrupted Magnus. He continued to ramble, 'We're taking it up the mountains to give to some friends: the reindeer herders—the Mountain Sami. We like to give them a gift of stockfish. Before they leave.'

Too much information, thought Erik.

From where he was standing, the German cast an eye over the load of fish. He looked carefully at Magnus and then to Erik. He frowned. Erik could almost sense the tension in Magnus; he needed to divert the German quickly.

'Do you want to try some?' asked Erik. 'It's such a delicacy.' He beckoned the German closer, encouraging him to peer into the basket. Erik held his nerve.

The soldier leaned forward and sniffed the contents, the

radio only inches from his face. But the putrid smell must have quickly filled his nostrils and swept into his lungs. He was overcome with horror, as if he'd been gassed. His face clenched, his eyes watered, and he started to cough and retch violently. His reaction was met with a bellow of laughter from the group of Germans watching. They jeered and shouted insults at their colleague. These boys had made him look a fool.

The German threw Erik and Magnus a look of disgust.

'No. I would not,' he said curtly, whipping out a white handkerchief and holding it to his nose.

'Okay,' beamed Erik. 'It's not for everyone.'

Erik kept his face as straight as possible as the German marched away still complaining and coughing.

The clip clop of the hooves was a comforting rhythm as they wound their way out of the village and up the hill. Finally, they allowed themselves a moment to relax.

Erik shook his head, smiling. 'I keep seeing his face when he put his nose in the basket!'

Magnus giggled. 'Can you believe he did that?'.

Erik copied the German's screwed up face, eyes protruding; he grabbed his neck and pretended to be choking. Magnus howled with laughter. Erik hadn't heard Magnus laugh for a long time and he smiled broadly at his friend. Perhaps Magus had forgotten what it felt like, and what it sounded like. He was laughing so hard now that tears ran down his cheeks. It was tricky to know whether he was happy or sad; the tears kept flowing. It was uncomfortable seeing Magnus sob.

'It is going to be fine. Magnus,' he said reassuringly. 'And we are doing something so important here. So significant. Be proud of yourself, and of your family.'

Magnus looked calmer. He wiped his face on his sleeve. The only sound now was of the hooves and the fish swinging and thumping on the boys' hips as they walked.

'I thought my father was never coming back, you know,' Magnus offered, 'the other night.' He shook his head despairingly. 'It's as though we live on the edge all the time. Most nights I can't sleep because I think I hear footsteps coming. As though they're coming to take him away. And then they really did. One day they'll take him and...' Tears once more flowed down his cheeks.

The gentle slope above the village was now a steep climb as they headed into the mountains. The horse walked with sturdy steps, but the boys' legs ached as they clambered up the narrow, rocky paths. A light covering of snow shimmered on the ground and the air felt clearer and sharper.

'How much further?' groaned Magnus. But no sooner had he asked, there was the sound of distant drumming.

'What's that noise?' said Magnus, frowning.

'That, my friend,' replied Erik, 'is the sound of a thousand reindeer.'

CHAPTER TWENTY-ONE

The Mountain Sami

NORWAY 1944

Taking the last few steps to the top of the peak, Erik and Magnus stood bent over, panting and trying to catch their breath.

'That last bit was murder,' gasped Magnus. 'Just murder.' Sweat ran in rivers down his forehead and the back of his neck.

Erik stood up and looked out. Before them, the snow-capped mountains had parted, creating an expansive plateau that thrummed with the sound of hundreds of reindeer. Lavvu tents were dotted along the edges as the Sami moved amongst their herd with dogs.

Erik patted Magnus on the back and signalled out over the view ahead.

'Look!' he exclaimed. 'We've made it!'

Magnus looked overwhelmed. 'What are they doing?'

'Getting ready to leave, by the looks of things,' said Erik.

The reindeer that wandered freely around the island all summer were being gathered together. They would soon head down the mountains as one huge herd. Then they would make the arduous swim across the freezing fjord, before starting the long journey inland to their home for the winter months. Erik and Magnus ambled down towards the plateau, leading the horse carefully.

'Erik!' yelled a voice. A girl, about their age, moved confidently through the reindeer towards them. Her face peered through the antler branches that were silhouetted in the now dusky light. She wore a neat cap and a warm tunic and boots made of reindeer skins; a bright plaid shawl was knotted around her shoulders.

'Inga!' shouted Erik. He turned to Magnus. 'She's my cousin.'

'Oh!' said Magnus. 'I didn't know...' he said quietly, but his voice trailed off.

'What are you doing here?' she asked.

'What did she say?' asked Magnus. 'Erik, do you speak...?' he began. But then he stopped. Erik spoke over him.

'We've brought you some stockfish!' Erik replied, in the same Sami language. Magnus looked confused.

'Thank you,' replied Inga and she added, 'I've no meat for you and your family because we're leaving soon. If I'd known you were coming...'

'No, don't worry,' said Erik shaking his head. 'Inga, I need your help. We need a cave. A safe cave. The dry stockfish here is for you, but this,' he said, pointing to the festering damp fish in the basket, 'is covering something we need to hide.' He paused. She raised her eyebrows. 'From the Nazis,' he added.

Inga's face dropped into a frown and she leant in to look. The smell caught her nostrils and she winced, clutching her fingers to her nose. 'A good hiding place!' she laughed.

Magnus smiled too; this needed no translation.

'I have a good hiding place too,' she smiled, and beckoned them over to the rocky hillside shrouded in trees. 'And the dogs will love the smelly fish!'

'You are leaving tomorrow?' Erik asked.

'We should have left this island two weeks ago!' said Inga desperately. Her expression was fraught and a look of fear flashed across her face. 'But we've had word that the Nazis have done terrible things to our home, and to our people.'

'What do you mean?' asked Erik.

'The Nazis are retreating from the north, that is for sure, but as they go, they are spreading as much fire and destruction as they can.' Her eyes filled with tears. 'They are wicked, wicked men. We hear there is nothing left. But the reindeer can't stay here over winter.' She looked back across the herd and up to the mountains circling them. 'The snow is beginning to fall. There will be no food for them here. So we must go. But what we will encounter on our journey...?' She shook her head. 'And what we shall find when we get there...?' She shuddered and wiped away a tear. 'We must go,' she said.

Erik translated for Magnus. This news spurred them on.

'The cave?' said Erik. 'It's for the good of us all.'

'Up there,' said Inga, pointing to a large break in some rocks. 'If you clamber up, there's a gap. Enough for you to fit through. And below is a cave. You can only enter it through that gap; it's not something you would stumble upon. No one will ever find whatever it is you are hiding.' She didn't ask what it was they were concealing.

'Thanks, Inga,' said Erik, handing her armfuls of the dried stockfish from the side of the basket. 'For your journey,' he added.

Inga pointed to the wet fish on top of the radio. 'If you tip that out, my dogs will gladly lap it up.' she laughed. 'It will make a nice change for them!'

Erik obliged and, with a few whistles, Inga's family's dogs appeared and soon the putrid fish was gone.

Tying up the horse, the boys set about their next challenge. They unwrapped the radio and in small stages, passing it carefully between them, they managed to get to the top. They cautiously looked down into the cave below; it was relatively shallow. Erik clambered inside first, and then Magnus cautiously passed the suitcase down. It was a tight space with enough room for one, maybe two, people. Once inside it was pitch black. They made the journey again, this time with the cumbersome battery.

Just as Inga had said, from the plateau, the cave was completely hidden. Erik committed its position to memory. He would be back later to act as a guide for the agent who was to operate the radio.

'You almost seem at home up here,' remarked Magnus, as they said their goodbyes. 'I didn't know you could, I mean you were...' he began. Magnus looked bewildered and confused, as though he didn't really know where to begin. 'I think maybe there are many things about you, Erik, that I didn't know,' he said.

'My grandmother was from the Mountain Sami,' Erik said quickly. He paused and looked back wistfully across the plateau. 'So I suppose you could say, I *am* at home up here,' he added, quietly.

With their mission accomplished, they set off on their journey back down the mountainside. The radio was safely hidden away. All Erik had to do now was wait.

Chapter Twenty-Two

Aboard The Northern Light
The North Sea 2014

'Gus, take over here, will you? I'm just going below for a couple of minutes,' said Finn.

It was now several hours since they had left Lerwick. The swell and pull of the sea rocked *The Northern Light*, making her creak with each gentle strain. It wasn't a rough sea, but it was there, softly teasing and tugging.

'I'll skipper, right?' said Gus, as more of a statement than a question. Finn felt a surge of irritation, he didn't really know why. But he conceded that it was the obvious decision. He'd not been coming out on the boat for long, while Gus was cool-headed and always seemed to know what to do. Besides, he felt too ropey to argue. He felt dizzy. The adrenalin rush of the escape from the Nazi was now replaced by another familiar, and wholly unpleasant, sensation. The reek of the diesel and wafts from the fish room down below, yet to be cleaned from the previous trip, all added to the nausea that grew in intensity.

'Aye,' Finn muttered in agreement. 'Of course.'

'Nae bother,' Gus said, patting him on the back. 'Take your time.'

'I'm gonna check what's in the stores, you know?' Finn added.

Finn shuffled past Olde.

'Are you okay, Finn?' said Olde.

'Yup,' lied Finn, as he dropped down the steep steps to the cabin below. He felt terrible, as if his stomach was trying to escape his body. Saliva oozed into his mouth.

'He's new to this, I suppose,' said Olde. 'Takes time to get past the sickness.'

After his visit to the bathroom, Finn staggered back up the ladder, conscious that the sounds of his retching would have echoed up from the bowels of the boat. His face was twisted in disgust. 'It's stinking down there,' he complained. 'Nothing's been cleaned out since the last trip.'

'It's grim,' agreed Gus.

'What's in the stores?' Gus enquired, clearly attempting to ignore the stench drifting up the stairs.

'We've got a few pies in the freezer,' Finn said, between long, lingering intakes of breath, 'and chips, of course. And there are loads of Pot Noodles and baked beans in the cupboards. Nae milk though,' he added with a hiccup. He closed his eyes, as though composing himself enough to get the next sentence out without belching, or worse. 'But there's enough food to keep us going for a couple of days or so, anyway.' He turned and staggered out onto the deck, gripping the railings. His head bowed, swaying with the motion of the boat.

Gus blurted suddenly, 'Oh my God! What about Gran? The Nazi guy will have gone straight round to the house! We have to get help to her, alert the police or something!'

Olde had a look of steady calm. 'They'll not bother with Anna,' he said. 'They know where we're going. They won't want him to waste another minute in Shetland. That I am sure of. Don't worry.'

The steady pulse of the engine filled the silence. The magnitude of what they were doing was too great even to talk.

'We'll get you sorted up here in the wheelhouse, Olde,' said Gus, now sticking with the practicalities. 'We can squash a mattress down on the floor and, you know, we can bring a bucket up here too. Well, it's more than just a bucket—it's pretty steady. We can secure it into the corner over there for you.'

Olde nodded. The stairs to the depths of the boat were too steep; he would have to muck in, and indeed, muck out.

'You're not missing anything there, Olde,' grumbled Finn from out on the deck. 'The toilet's bogging.'

Olde rolled his eyes.

'And that pipe in there is totally ropey, Gus,' Finn continued, sounding extremely ratty. 'It needs fixed before we end up sinking.'

'I can at least take my turn at the controls,' Olde added, ignoring Finn.

Gus nodded vaguely, 'Aye, Olde, that'd be grand.' Gus shifted his attention to the small screens in front of him. He examined the plotters and the GPS that would help them find their way.

'So, Gus, have you planned the route?' asked Olde.

'Piece of cake, Olde. Piece of cake,' smiled Gus, his voice a little quiet. 'As long as the weather plays ball.'

It wasn't until much later, when dusk turned the sea to a glimmering black, and oil platforms lit up like Christmas trees studded their route, that Gus spoke to his great-grandfather while Finn sat at the controls.

'What happened with *Tirpitz*, Olde?' he asked tentatively. 'I mean, you know, what it's all about? I know it's frustrating for you that we don't know and we're ignorant. But...' he stopped himself and stared at the old man in the dim light of the wheelhouse.

Olde sighed.

'It was the only way. We had to do what we had to do,' he said quietly and looked down. 'During the war we had to look at the bigger picture. And that meant human sacrifice. You will understand soon,' he said grimly.

Gus stared curiously at his great-grandfather, but didn't ask any more questions.

'They'll know now,' Olde added. And Gus noticed a twinkle in his eye.

'What? Who?' Gus asked, confused.

'The staff. At the home, they'll know I'm missing. And they'll know you are too. The search will be on.'

Gus glanced back nervously. He stared out along their watery trail, to see if they were being followed. Then he shook his head.

'Watching your back, eh?' said Olde. 'I remember doing that many moons ago when I journeyed from Norway to Shetland; every boat, every plane, was a threat.'

But there was no going back now.

Whatever they had started, they had to finish.

Chapter Twenty-Three

The Cave

Norway 1944

Erik lay on his bed, eyes wide and alert. He had opened the window wide to let the crisp, cold air gently waft around his room. It was a still, calm day. Outside, seabirds screeched and called and the water gently lapped along the rocks below their croft. The chickens were scratching around outside and there was an occasional bleat from their goats. But all Erik could concentrate on was the distant thrum of *Tirpitz* echoing up the fjord. It was a sickening pulse. After the most recent attack on *Tirpitz*, Erik realised she hadn't been seriously damaged because soon after, when all was quiet again, the pulse returned. He closed his eyes. With every beat of its engines, images flashed into his mind. He could see fear and terror in the eyes of people he knew and loved. Erik felt a sudden surge of impatience for change. But all he could do was wait for the signal that had been agreed with Per Johansen, and then he would act. But how long would he have to wait? It had been several days now since they had delivered the radio.

There was no school as the teacher rotated his lessons to children around the remote areas. He couldn't go to

Hans. And Per had insisted that he should not visit until he had further information from the Resistance. Erik sat up, his head in his hands. He shut the window, but he could still hear it. The heartbeat of evil penetrated his bedroom walls and his head. Erik jumped out of bed. He needed to do something, anything to keep his mind occupied. He got dressed, pulling on a large, heavy jumper, and wandered downstairs. All was quiet. His father would have set off hours ago to go fishing, and his mother would be out tending the animals. She would be expecting him to go outside and help, but he had bigger concerns. Just to keep her happy, he would take some tools with him and tell her he was off to mend a few fences on his travels.

Erik grabbed a torch from the porch and a spade and hammer from the toolshed. He walked down to the shore, waving to his mother as he went. She shouted something to him, but he pretended he couldn't hear. At the water's edge, he freed the small dinghy they kept tied to the rocks. He pushed it out, jumped in at the last minute, and started to heave on the oars. Erik kept close to the shoreline and rowed towards the mouth of the fjord. The sea was clear and still and the oars sliced and slipped below the surface of the crystal water. Every so often, he swung round to check his direction, now rowing more carefully. He soon became aware of another boat approaching; it was going relatively fast. Erik stopped rowing and waited. It was grey with a streak of red: the Nazi flag, prominent at the stern. Three men stood on the deck, with binoculars scouring the coastline; it was a patrol boat. Erik felt a shiver down his spine and sat frozen, gripping the oars. But the boat swept past, leaving him to bob and rock in its wake. Soon, it was a tiny spot in the distance, but the red of the flag lingered on, like a splash of fresh blood on the landscape.

Erik shook off the fear that had enveloped him momentarily, and picked up the steady rhythm of the oars once more. He approached the caves—the caves where he and Magnus had witnessed the Germans unloading something a few weeks earlier. He needed to see what it was they had been so keen to conceal. Looking up above the shoreline, he pinpointed where he and Magnus had been hiding—it had to be the cave directly below. There was a small pebble beach in front of it and he clambered out, securing the boat by looping the rope over a rock.

He lowered his head and stepped in cautiously, shining the torch. Erik knew this cave well. He had spent many hours exploring it as a young child. From the outside, a small hole was visible and yet, when you entered, you encountered a spacious, rocky cavern. The ground was covered in fine pebbles, but Erik didn't have to stoop. He could move around quite freely. And so he began to investigate with his torch, examining floor to ceiling. Nothing seemed out of place. There were no obvious signs of anyone recently having been in the cave. He was distracted by the beauty of the room when he heard a noise. He froze.

To his alarm, he realised he could hear footsteps on the gravel outside. *Someone was coming!* He quickly switched off his torch and crouched down, pressing himself into the wall of the cave. He glanced out and saw the silhouette of a man against the shoreline. But with the light behind him, Erik couldn't see his face. A chill of horror ran up his spine.

Erik's mind raced. He tried to curb his breathing, but with the dinghy outside for all to see, whoever it was knew he was here. Had the patrol boat followed him? He cursed himself for his own stupidity. Per Johansen's words—"we will make a good spy of you yet"—now seemed ridiculous. The footsteps moved into the cave and he heard a click. The bright beam of a torch searched high and low, getting ever nearer to Erik's face. The sharp edge of the rocks dug into his shoulder blades as he pressed himself further and further back. Then the light switched off abruptly and the silhouette turned and walked steadily out of the cave. Erik was still frozen to the spot. He remained still, until his heartbeat calmed and his breathing returned to normal. Finally, his tense body relaxed and he lifted his back away from the rocks, but he still didn't leave his corner. He listened intently, but could hear only the sea and its gentle ripples outside. Slowly, he crept towards the light, stopping every so often to scrutinise every snatch of sound that might suggest someone was out there; that someone was waiting for him.

Eventually, Erik made it to the mouth of the cave. He peered around the edge of the rocks, but all that was there was his dinghy. Something else caught his attention; it was the unmistakable scent of tobacco. Just as he sank down, retreating backwards quietly, he heard a clear voice,

'Are you going to wait in there forever, Erik?'

Chapter Twenty-Four

Cave Diggers

Norway 1944

Erik was gripped first by terror, but then relief, as he realised he knew exactly who was out there. It was Hans.

He shuffled back outside sheepishly. Round the corner from the cave, Hans was sitting on a rock looking out over the fjord, casually smoking a cigarette. He looked at Erik, a half-smile twisting his face. Erik walked sheepishly towards him, and Hans let out a long stream of smoke through his nostrils.

'What were you thinking?' he said.

'I dunno,' said Erik. 'Curiosity got the better of me, I suppose.'

'Well, lucky for you I was here to keep watch, eh? For goodness' sake, Erik! There are Nazi patrol boats going up and down this fjord all the time. The world's most powerful battleship is sitting just up there! Or had you forgotten that fact?'

Erik reddened. He took the scolding he received from Hans; it was well-deserved.

'Now, let's get this dinghy out of sight,' Hans said. 'And then we can get back to finding out what secrets this cave is hiding.'

They dragged the boat ashore, up onto the grass, where they hid it behind a clump of bushes, before heading back into the cave.

They searched the cave methodically, until Hans spotted a corner at the very back that seemed unnatural compared to the rest of the rock formation. A build-up of large rocks appeared to be crammed into a space or opening. Hans began to pull loose rocks away. Some were small and could be shifted away easily, but others needed to be hauled out. Erik joined him and together they worked their hands around the boulders, until a largish hole was revealed. It was big enough for a man to climb through. Hans shone the torch inside and inspected the space beyond.

'This is it!' he announced. 'I can see wooden crates.'

He reached in and pulled hard. The box was brutally heavy and Erik reached his hands through the small gap to help heave it out.

'What's inside this damn box?' exclaimed Erik. 'Rocks?'

'Go and grab that hammer that you brought in the dinghy, Erik,' said Hans.

When Erik returned, Hans dug the claw end of the hammer deep under the lid of the first crate. Using a lever action, he pulled back and forth, his knee resting on the edge. Then, with a splintering of wood, the lid was released. Instantly, the torch reflected back its glittering contents: a row of gold bars shimmered brilliantly, defiantly in the gloom of the cave.

'Gold?' said Erik. 'Is it real?' He picked up a bar; it was surprisingly cool.

'Dirty gold, you mean,' muttered Hans. 'And yes, it's real

114

alright. Don't touch it, Erik. It must have been transported here by *Tirpitz* and now they're hiding it. Or someone is hiding it because *Tirpitz* is a target—or because the Nazis know their time is nearly up. When the right time comes, they'll be back for it.'

Hans moved away from the box, as if it were contaminated, and crouched at the far end of the cave. Erik studied the bar in his hand; he traced his finger over the outstretched eagle, imprinted on its surface, a swastika in its talons. Then he placed it back in the box.

'Why did you call it dirty gold?' asked Erik.

'That gold is from the melted down watches, rings and bracelets of thousands of Jews!' Hans spat out the words. 'They even took the gold from their teeth. Animals,' he added, his voice breaking with anger.

Erik was quiet. Hans lowered his head.

'I'm Jewish, Erik,' Hans said. 'I'm what the Nazis call a Mischling—a "half breed". My grandmother was a Jew, but my mother kept it a secret to protect us all. So that we wouldn't be sent away. Sent away to certain death, like the rest of her family—forced onto cattle trains to camps that are worse than hell. When I joined the army,' he explained, 'and trained as a radar operator, they found out that I had Jewish relatives. They investigated my family tree and I was deemed to be a "Mischling of the second degree". Because I had only one Jewish grandparent, I was allowed to continue my job. But I am forbidden to marry a Jew. If I do, I join others in those hell-hole concentration camps.'

A silence fell between them.

'To deny who you are, who your family is,' said Erik

115

earnestly, 'or even to keep it a secret because of what others might think, is a terrible thing. But to see your family taken away or killed...' He trailed away. 'It's too awful, Hans.'

Hans, now deep in his own thoughts leant against the wall of the cave.

'Let's get rid of this,' Erik said, firmly. 'Let's tip it into the sea!'

'Someone might see us. It's too dangerous,' said Hans. 'But we're not leaving it here for them to neatly collect when it suits them.' He ran his fingers through his hair. 'But as soon as we leave this cave, we risk being seen or stopped and searched.' Hans spoke his thoughts aloud.

'So if it's too risky to leave, then let's re-hide it here!' said Erik. 'They'll not stop to search the cave itself when they realise it's been taken!'

Hans listened and nodded. Before he'd had a chance to respond, Erik shot out of the cave and returned with the shovel he'd stashed in the dinghy.

Together, they scoured the cave. They quickly found an area towards the back with soft, loose pebbles. They started to shovel furiously. They took turns to dig, the other helping to scoop back the stones. Hans speared the shovel into the ground with an angry force. Sweat rolled down his face and dripped onto the stones below, but his determination and pace didn't falter. Down and down into the hole he dug, until they hit rock. Hours passed as they continued to dig outwards, transforming the back of the cave into a sunken trench. Finally, they dragged the crates, like coffins to the grave. Then they shovelled back the layers of gritty sand and stones. Once covered, they took time to analyse the surface, smoothing the top layer so that it looked untouched. Hans disappeared outside and returned with armfuls of identical sized stones from the pebble beach. Erik did the same. In and out they staggered, with more and more armfuls, until it looked as though no man had set foot in that cave.

Hans pulled a large piece of misshapen wood out of his pocket. One L-shaped arm of a swastika was printed on its surface.

'What's that?' asked Erik.

'A piece of the lid that splintered off,' said Hans. He placed the scrap of wood carefully by the hole where the gold had been hidden. 'So that there is no doubt that it's been taken,' he added.

'Tell no one, Erik. Not a soul. Not even Magnus. No one. Do you hear me?' Hans looked troubled. Distracted even. He rubbed his brow. 'Nothing good could ever come of that gold,' he said quietly.

They emerged from the cave into the dusk of mid-afternoon and retrieved the dinghy. Erik waved to Hans as he set off rowing back along the fjord to the croft.

He hoped and prayed that no one was watching him from the shore.

CHAPTER TWENTY-FIVE

The Agent

NORWAY 1944

Erik pulled the dinghy back onto the shore, and had begun to walk uphill towards his farmhouse when he heard a shout,

'Hey, Erik!' It was Magnus. 'Where've you been? I've been searching all over the village for you.'

'Why, Magnus? What's happened?'

Magnus grabbed Erik, looking all around. Although they were quite alone, Magnus still whispered the words into Erik's ear.

'My father has had word. The agent is to return to the village tonight, Erik. Tonight.'

Erik nodded. An intense look of understanding passed between the two boys. Then Magnus turned and ran up the hill, on to the track to head back towards the village.

Dressed in his darkest clothes, Erik left the house just after midnight. It was a bitterly cold, clear night. He checked his watch. He was to meet the agent—a man—that was all he'd been told, in the village graveyard, at quarter past. He climbed on his bike, making sure to cycle in the blackest of shadows. He carried his torch, but wouldn't need to use it until he was well away from the village. The moon radiated a bright beam and the soft green glow of the Northern Lights flickered and danced in the vast sky above.

Erik turned up the high road, being careful to make as little sound as possible as he neared the village. The old church with its ancient graveyard stood looking over its parish below. And there, leaning against a headstone, was a shadowy figure.

Stepping off his bike, Erik walked through the gateway cautiously. He didn't know what to say. Or whether he should say anything. They hadn't agreed a secret whistle or coded greeting.

'Hello?' whispered Erik.

'Erik?' answered the man quietly. Erik frowned; there was something familiar about his voice.

As he approached him, Erik screwed his eyes to focus on the face in the dark. Then it dawned on him—this man, in the graveyard, was his teacher.

'Mr. Olsen?' he stammered.

'Sshhhhhh! Lower your voice, boy,' warned Olsen.

'But Mr. Olsen,' whispered Erik, trying to unravel his confusion. 'What are you doing here?'

'Meeting you, boy,' replied Olsen.

Realisation hit Erik with a sharp jolt: Olsen *was* the agent. He felt like a fool. It all slotted into place. As a peripatetic teacher, his job involved travelling to several schools. He was an ideal candidate to work as an agent with the Resistance as he could move around quite easily without raising any Nazi eyebrows. And popping in and out of Per Johansen's shop wouldn't seem out of place, either.

'We've not got much time, Erik,' whispered Olsen, reaching into his bag for a torch. Erik hid his bike amongst the gravestones. They set off quickly up the mountain path that Erik and Magnus had taken days ago with the radio.

Olsen and Erik didn't speak on their journey. Per Johansen had already explained to Erik that it was best not to talk. Trading information, even on a small scale, could be dangerous. To know too much could seal the fate of other men—if you were captured and tortured. Silence, he had explained, was the safest option, but Erik felt too awkward to chat to his teacher anyway; he spoke only when he had to.

Eventually, they made it to the high ground, which now echoed with an eerie silence. The Sami were gone, now making their arduous journey for miles across water and land to their winter pastures. Erik led Olsen down into the empty plateau, the occasional screech of a bird making them jump.

Erik stopped and shone his torch along the rocky hillside.

'There!' he breathed, shining the beam on the break in the rocks. Together they scrambled to the mouth of the cave. Looking inside, it seemed, in the dark, a deeper drop. But they worked their way down, one shining the light for the other.

They set Olsen's torch on a rocky shelf within the cave, and Erik perched on a rock while Olsen opened the suitcase. He passed Erik a bundle of tightly wrapped cables.

'Head out of the cave, unwind this and throw the end up into a nearby tree,' he said.

Erik looked at him blankly.

'It's the aerial,' he added. 'Quickly!'

Erik clambered back up and unwound one end, feeding it back into the murky depths below. Then he flung the other end until it caught onto a branch. When he got back, Olsen attached the other end tightly into the radio. Other wires and cables were pulled out and plugged in, then Olsen slipped a pair of headphones onto his head. He reached into his pocket for a notebook and pencil, and began twisting and adjusting the dials in front of him. He checked his watch and sat still for several minutes. Then he checked it again. Finally, he started tapping with a small instrument set into the radio. He was typing in Morse code. He stopped, and in the stillness Erik could tell he was listening now, his face deep in concentration and, with a sense of urgency, he began scribbling furiously into his notebook.

Then, Olsen started to tap back and Erik waited. Abruptly, Olsen stopped, pulled off his headphones and swiftly unplugged the wires, winding everything together.

'Go and pull the aerial back in,' ordered Olsen. 'We need to hurry. Listen carefully to what I'm about to tell you, Erik, this information involves you. The British intend another attempt on *Tirpitz* in a matter of hours, and Hans has a plan.'

'What kind of plan?' asked Erik, as he scrambled out of the cave. He yanked on the aerial wire until it dropped to the ground, and threw the end back down to Olsen.

'The Germans have stationed fighter planes nearby, at an airbase called Bardufoss,' explained Olsen, as Erik reappeared beside him. 'Those planes are there so that if the British launch an attack, they can defend *Tirpitz*.'

'So how on earth is Hans going to stop them?' asked Erik.

'It's all about timing. A simple case of timing,' said Olsen snapping shut the suitcase.

Erik frowned. Olsen looked at his watch.

'Go now, don't wait for me, and deliver the message to Hans. We're anticipating an attack at around 8.30am,' he said.

Erik groaned.

'Getting through the village with my bike in tow is not easy,' he said. 'The place is swarming with Germans. What if they stop me? What do I say?' Erik hoped Olsen would provide him with an easy answer. 'Maybe I should borrow the dinghy and row up to the radar?'

Olsen took in a deep breath and looked up to the starry sky above. He shook his head.

'The fjord will be swarming with patrol boats and search lights. Particularly at night. They would stop you for sure.'

Erik nodded. He tried to think of some other way but conceded to himself there was no easy solution.

'Erik,' said Olsen. 'You must do your duty tonight, whatever the cost. Engage in any act of sabotage if it's to further our cause. Look into yourself and find all the courage you can muster.'

Erik stared into the dark at the outline of his schoolmaster.

'Go. And get that message to Hans. You have a chance here to help bring about an end to all of this.'

Erik swallowed. He stood up decisively and set off, deftly climbing to the top of the cave.

'Good luck!' called Olsen. But Erik was already running and scrambling across the empty plateau.

Chapter Twenty-Six

The Dream

The North Sea 2014

'Olde?' said Finn, turning to look at his great-grandfather. He was asleep, sitting up in his chair, obviously having some sort of dream. But then Olde cried out. Finn jumped. He pushed his chair back from the controls and stood, facing Olde. Sweat had formed in beads across his wrinkled forehead, his sunken eyes were clamped shut. His mouth worked and twitched as he struggled awkwardly in his seat. His fists were clenched and jerked outwards.

'Olde,' Finn raised his voice a little and hesitantly reached out a hand to touch his shoulder. He was completely still now and his face relaxed, the creases smoothed, his eyes at peace. Finn shook him a little. Was he still breathing?

'Olde,' he shouted. Still nothing. But then the old man's eyes snapped open and he took in a gasp of air, filling his lungs. He tried to focus, and searched around, looking confused. Then he reached up to rub his brow which was drenched in sweat.

'You had me worried there, Olde!' said Finn, continuing to stare warily into his great-grandfather's eyes. 'You were in a deep sleep—I thought you'd never wake up!' As soon as the words were out of his mouth, he realised how bad that sounded. He bit his lip and hoped Olde wouldn't be offended.

'Thought I'd popped my clogs, eh?' mumbled Olde, still recovering.

'You seemed a bit, well, stressed. You know, like you were

having a bad dream,' said Finn.

'I'm fine, boy,' said Olde, dismissing Finn's concern.

'You called out,' Finn added.

'Did I?' said Olde cautiously. 'What did I say?'

'Dunno,' mumbled Finn.

'Just havering was I? Not making any sense?'.

'Maybe,' nodded Finn. Then he added, 'But it sounded like you were talking a different language: not Norwegian—I hear you and Gran talk in Norwegian all the time. Sounded more like German.'

'Oh?' said Olde looking down at his fingers. 'How strange.'

Finn continued to stare at Olde before returning his attention to the boat's dashboard and fiddling with a few dials. He glanced back at Olde from time to time.

'What was your dream about?' He threw the question at his great-grandfather casually.

Olde closed his eyes.

'It's a dream I've had many times before,' he explained. 'It's about drowning.'

Finn frowned and curled the edges of his lip. He didn't let his great-grandfather see his expression, but he wished he hadn't asked.

'I'm trapped, you see,' Olde said quietly, 'trapped inside an upturned ship, inside a compartment. The water is rising and I can't find a way out,' he explained, somehow trying to make sense of the images. 'Icy water laps around my shoulders; the tide is rising. The darkness is terrifying and fear has drained me of all strength,' Olde rubbed his temples, still lost in the horrors. 'The water is thick and oily,' he continued. 'The stench of diesel fills my lungs. All around me, men are dying and screaming. Some float face down, already dead. I bang my fists on the sides, desperate that someone, *anyone*, might hear me. And then the water is lapping around my lips. I press my head against the ceiling that was once the floor but the water still rises and swills into my mouth. Soon every crevice of the compartment will be full of water. And then a strange thing happens,' he looked over to Finn. 'I feel an overwhelming calmness. I let go. The water covers my nose and face, my arms float outwards and a sleep comes over me, a long endless sleep.'

Finn was silent. He didn't know what to say.

'I always do wake up, though,' said Olde.

Finn couldn't be sure, but Olde's eyes were glistening, as if with tears.

'That, Finn, was what I was dreaming about,' he said curtly.

'Right,' said Finn. 'Braaly heavy, eh?'

Olde nodded. 'Yes, "braaly heavy", as you say. But my dream is just that: only a dream, thank God.' He reached up to quickly wipe his eyes before reaching for his glasses.

What had Olde just said? His great-grandfather's face was grim and twisted in distress. What was he on about, Finn wondered? Was he just trying to shock him? Or was this something to do with this *Tirpitz* ship? He was hard to understand. Finn shook his head. Olde was a bit like a jigsaw puzzle. Except the pieces were released slowly—one at a time.

Dawn was now breaking and the boat had found a steady rhythm. Finn yawned and stretched.

'Why don't you go and get some sleep?' offered Olde, standing up. 'I can take over here—at least for an hour or two, until Gus is awake.'

Finn was unsure; he was worried about leaving Olde alone. But his great-grandfather was already at the wheel.

The mere suggestion of sleep had kick-started Finn's exhaustion, and he could feel the pull of his body to close his eyes.

'Okay, Olde,' Finn said, adding in spite of himself, 'You're sure you know what you're doing?'

Olde threw him a look that needed no reply.

Finn nodded backing away towards the steps.

'Shout if you need us?' And he was gone, like a rabbit down a hole, leaving his great-grandfather alone in the wheelhouse.

CHAPTER TWENTY-SEVEN

Kristoffer

NORWAY 1944

Checking his watch, Erik made it back to the churchyard. It was 3am. If he pedalled fast, it shouldn't take him long to reach Seal Point. And if Hans was at the billets, it would take even less time. There was no need for panic, he told himself. But still he felt a sense of burden with the information Olsen had given him; he was anxious to pass it on as soon as possible. He looked towards the village in its dark slumber. Ordinarily, it would have been so simple to creep through without being seen. Why did it seem so impassable tonight? The shriek of an owl in the trees behind him made him jump.

He gave himself a shake and retrieved his bike from the mossy graves in the churchyard. He pedalled slowly along the road. The houses were all clustered along one side, but there was a back path that he could take, to avoid being seen. The village hall was his main concern as there were always a couple of Nazi officers milling around outside. But as he approached the hall, he could hear laughter and voices. Music drifted out: the unmistakable beat of jazz. Erik carefully followed the back path to stay hidden. Curious as to what was going on inside, he placed his torch down and, resting his bike on the wall, he crept close to the building. He looked carefully through one of the windows—the blackout curtains hadn't even been drawn. The room was full of Germans; they were drinking and laughing. Some were dancing. Others were slumped on chairs, their uniforms loosened, their feet on the tables. What was he worrying about? These Germans weren't fit to walk down the street in a straight line, let alone quiz a boy as to where he was going in the middle of the night. These Germans were undisciplined! They didn't seem to care anymore. He turned to head back on his journey when he froze, his face illuminated by torchlight.

'Erik?' said a menacing voice. 'And what might you be doing here at this time?'

Erik couldn't see who spoke with the light shining in his eyes. But with a flick, it swung away from his face. Erik groaned. Kristoffer's sinister features were now glowing from the torch. Like a predator, he appeared excited with his find.

'I think you should come with me,' he said, roughly grabbing Erik's arm. Erik tried to pull away, but Kristoffer's fingers had an iron grip. 'Father will be very interested to hear you were wandering around, spying on the Germans.'

'I was not spying Kristoffer. Now let me go!'

Kristoffer dragged him onwards and let out a small laugh. 'I don't think so, Erik. Do you know what I think? I think you're up to something. With that radar operator. I've been watching you—and this proves it.'

'Proves what?' Erik snapped back, trying to shake his

arm free.

Kristoffer twisted Erik's arm up behind his back. Erik cried out in pain as Kristoffer marched on, pushing him towards the village hall.

'What are you taking me in here for?' said Erik.

'My father is in here, of course!' sneered Kristoffer. 'He's good friends with the officers.'

Erik felt nausea rising in his throat. Time was slipping away, and if taken inside he would undoubtedly be imprisoned, perhaps tortured. There was sweat on his brow as Kristoffer pushed him towards the door. He felt a surge of anger at himself for being caught so quickly. What an idiot he had been, lingering by the village hall. He tried to struggle and fight, but Kristoffer's strength was too much for him. Kristoffer laughed.

'You're pathetic, Erik. A pathetic, snivelling little kid.'

He reached for the door and pushed Erik inside. A wall of cigarette smoke greeted them and the sour smell of alcohol. Erik's glasses instantly steamed up, and unable to wipe them, he could only see through a foggy haze. The gramophone in the corner was fired up with swing music. The Germans all around were raucous and drunk. Erik felt sick. Kristoffer stood with his prey, but no one appeared to pay a blind bit of notice to him. Kristoffer marched Erik over to his father, who was slouched in the corner.

'Father, look who I found outside!'

His glasses clearing now, Erik looked into the ruddy face of the local policeman. His eyes were half shut and froth had settled in the corners of his thin mouth. He was drunk.

'Father!' yelled Kristoffer, giving the man a nudge. He

opened one eye and looked from his son to Erik. But he struggled to focus and gave up, firmly shutting his eye again.

Kristoffer looked desperately around the room. But not one German officer was fit to take his efforts to capture Erik seriously.

'This is ridiculous Kristoffer. Let me go!' complained Erik.

'What have you got there then?' said a voice. Both boys turned to see a man staggering towards them. He had the look of a maniac.

'Caught this one snooping around outside, Sir,' announced Kristoffer.

'Good work, boy,' said the German. 'Lock him in a room somewhere, Kristoffer. We'll deal with him later.'

'No!' shouted Erik. 'No! I haven't done anything wrong!'

Kristoffer hustled him towards a small staircase in the hall. Erik tried to resist the stairs, but Kristoffer gave him a shove and he fell forward, toppling down to the bottom. He smashed his head on the cold, hard floor.

'Get up!' shouted Kristoffer and kicked him with a tremendous thud.

Erik groaned as he became overwhelmed with pain; Kristoffer's boot had struck him hard in the kidneys. He coughed and tried to stand up. But with another enormous shove, Kristoffer pushed him into a small, dark room and slammed the door. With a click of the lock, he was a prisoner.

Kristoffer taunted him through the door. 'See you at school now!' he called as he headed back up the stairs.

Muffled music and laughter filtered down as Erik lay

curled up on the floor in the dark. He shut his eyes as the beat of the jazz pulsated. His head throbbed; he could feel blood trickling and sticking to the hairs on the side of his head. Tears welled up in his eyes. He'd ruined everything. He felt utterly defeated.

But as he lay wallowing, the words of Olsen echoed in his mind,

"You must do your duty tonight whatever the cost. Engage in any act of sabotage if it's to further our cause. Look into yourself and find all the courage you can muster..."

Erik opened his eyes and in the dark, the secrets of the room began to reveal themselves. And as they did so, a plan started to form in his mind.

CHAPTER TWENTY-EIGHT

Sabotage

NORWAY 1944

The only real light in the room came from under the door. It was faint, but enough to highlight outlines of various objects. Erik realised that he was in a store room or walk-in cupboard of some description.

He hauled himself up and fumbled around. Something brushed against his head. He reached up to touch it. It was a long piece of cord. Instinctively he pulled it, instantly lighting up the room. Around him were filing cabinets and shelves stacked with folders and papers. He swiftly checked his watch.

Erik moved over to the door and turned the handle. He had heard Kristoffer turn the key, but he had to check. It was certainly locked. Bending down, he squinted through the key hole. He let out a gasp. That idiot Kristoffer had left the key in the lock! Pressing his ear to the door, the only sounds were the muffled music and laughter from upstairs. He tried to see under the door but it was no use. There were no other signs of life. Erik decided to test the waters. Kristoffer was sure to bite—if he was outside the door.

'Kristoffer!' he shouted. 'Let me out, knucklehead!'

There was no reply.

'You've got sawdust for brains!' he pushed a little harder. But still there was no reply. He must be back outdoors on patrol. It was time to act fast. He remembered an old trick that Olsen had told them at school. Olsen was always mentioning ideas for their "general knowledge", but now he wondered if Olsen had deliberately wanted to educate his own youngsters in the art of everyday sabotage. This might just work, he told himself.

Erik carefully removed a file from the shelves and, spotting a paper clip, he plucked it from its snug location binding two sheets of paper. He unwound the clip and popped it between his teeth. Then he placed the sheets of paper on the floor right by the door. This was the moment of truth. Erik pushed the paper under the door, so that it was directly under the key on the other side. He waited tensely, half expecting a shout or the door to be thrown open. But nothing happened. He pressed on. Wiggling the paper clip into the lock he managed to push the key a little out of its position. Erik had to bend the wire in half to make it more solid. This did the job and the key dislodged and dropped to the floor. Slowly and carefully, Erik pulled the paper under the door, back into the cupboard. He held his breath, but sure enough, there, lying innocently on the paper, was the key! Erik couldn't believe his luck! He slid the key into the lock on his side of the door, and with a simple click he was a step closer to freedom. Erik felt an enormous sense of relief and excitement at his own ingenuity. But he couldn't escape yet for fear of being seen. He pushed his hand into his pocket and felt for a penny—now he had another trick up his sleeve, thanks to Olsen. Perhaps his classes weren't so boring after all.

Spying a wooden crate, he pulled it into the middle of the room. He tested his weight to make sure it would hold, and hoisted himself up to reach the light. Then he pulled the cord so that he was now in complete darkness. Erik stood for a second to centre himself so that he wouldn't lose his balance. Feeling his way carefully, using the sleeves of his jumper as a protective glove, he unscrewed the lightbulb. He searched his pocket again for the penny and placed it on the top of the lightbulb. Awkwardly, he now screwed the bulb back in place. Erik breathed heavily and his pulse pounded in his neck. He stepped off the box and shifted it back into its position. Everything was ready.

Erik closed his eyes for a second. And then, not wanting to linger too long in case fear overwhelmed him, he reached for the chord and pulled. Instantly, there was a loud bang. The bulb popped and the light from under the door had gone out. Shouts and cries from upstairs confirmed it—the village hall had been plunged into darkness. He opened the door cautiously. It was so dark that it was impossible to see anything. Erik closed the door behind him and re-locked it, sliding the key underneath. That would slow them down, he thought. Then he groped forward until he found the stairs.

He had to hurry as the drunken Germans would inevitably stagger down here to look for a fuse box. Erik scrambled up the stairs, listening intently for sounds of approaching footsteps. He had almost made it to the top when there was the sound of drunken mumblings. The low light of the moon outside lit up the silhouette of a man at the top of the stairs. Erik froze. He could see the man begin to descend, and he switched to the opposite side and crouched low. The German swayed as he tried to negotiate the stairs in his stupor. Each step was taken awkwardly, like a child who has just learnt to walk. Erik waited until he was level with him and quickly scrambled past.

At the top, he slipped through the main door without anyone seeing him. Erik had made it! He had to hope that Kristoffer wasn't still prowling around outside. He couldn't risk trying to retrieve his bike, and would have to continue on foot.

As he ran as light-footed as possible through the shadows, he vowed that he would somehow make Kristoffer pay for his cruelty. But that wasn't his priority tonight. Tonight he was an agent, a messenger and a saboteur. Tonight, he was part of the Resistance.

Chapter Twenty-Nine

The Gathering Storm

The Norwegian Sea 2014

Finn was in a heavy sleep. Lying on his back, his jaw slackened, his loud snores bellowed over the sound of the engine.

'Finn! What the hell are you doing down here?' yelled Gus.

Finn sat up on his elbows, dazed and bewildered.

'You left Olde in charge of the boat, you cretin? You left a ninety-one-year-old in charge of our boat?' yelled Gus, his face blazing.

Before Finn could answer, Gus had snatched up his boots and had scrabbled up the steep steps to the wheelhouse.

Finn sighed and rubbed his face. He swung himself out of his bunk, and grabbing his clothes on the way, followed Gus upstairs.

'Good morning, Gus,' said Olde glancing round. 'Something wrong?'

Gus ignored Olde and, still clearly fuming, checked around the controls on the dashboard. He looked at the screens and data in front of him.

'Where are we, Olde? What have you done?' he snapped.

Finn looked on anxiously, there was going to be trouble now.

'I've made a few tweaks, shall we say, to the route,' Olde said, staring out of the window. 'Lovely sunrise, don't you think?'.

'You shouldn't have done that,' Gus said quietly, turning to his brother, 'Finn, I thought we agreed I was skipper?'

Gus glared between his brother and great-grandfather.

'Right?'

'Calm down, Gus!' said Olde. 'I can manage to pilot the boat for a bit. It's only been an hour or so. Don't blame Finn. It was my idea. Thought I could help out a bit.'

Gus's face was red. He leaned over his great-grandfather once more and began resetting the route.

'Eh, Gus, hang on a minute,' interrupted Olde, 'I managed to tune into the Norwegian shipping forecast. Sounds like there's a bit of bother with storms, so I thought I'd alter the route a bit to keep us out of trouble.'

'I had the route all planned. No offence, Olde, but you...'

'Don't know what I'm doing?' Olde volunteered, anger creeping into his voice, 'Am just an old coffin dodger? I worked on boats for years, Gus. I know a fair bit.'

'Aye, Olde,' said Gus, his tone sing-song and patronising, 'but that was a wee while ago, you know. It's dangerous stuff out here.'

Olde shifted out of his chair. Finn shook his head in disbelief at his brother. But chipping in would fuel Gus's stubbornness. Instead, he nibbled on the stumps of his fingernails.

'I'm going out on deck for a bit of fresh air,' Olde said. 'Now I see that you think I'm next to useless, I'll get out of your way.'

Olde passed Finn and put a hand firmly and affectionately onto his shoulder.

'Thanks, Finn, for having a bit of belief in the old man,' he said, adding bitterly, 'You'd think Gus didn't know that I've been in these waters before. Many times. In times far more dangerous than now.'

Finn gave him a weak, apologetic smile.

Gus, clearly wound up, immediately and stubbornly set the boat back on the original route. Finn couldn't hide his irritation with his brother. Gus took his role as skipper seriously and wasn't about to share his decision-making. But it was all so over the top. Once, he'd said that a skipper's dithering weakness could lead to disaster. Or was it their father who had said that? But Gus needed to chill out. It was hard to avoid each other on such a small vessel, but Olde was right to stay outside on the deck for as long as possible.

Eventually, Finn appeared beside Olde on the deck, with a cup of tea.

'Here you go, Olde,' he said awkwardly.

They stood side by side in silence. Finn had no idea what to say to make it right; his brother had been an idiot.

'It seems as if history is just something you read about. But real experience is invisible to the young,' said Olde, as he looked out to the expanse of ocean.

Finn glanced at his great-grandfather, who was now standing bolt upright, squinting as he looked out to sea. Something in the distance had caught Olde's eye.

'Finn, go and grab that pair of binoculars would you?' he said calmly.

Finn obliged. He could sense Olde's wariness.

Olde looked through the thick lenses.

'What is it, Olde?' asked Finn.

Olde pointed his gnarly finger. There it sat innocently on the horizon. A squall line was brooding ahead. A white line nestled neatly on a black, black sky.

'We've got trouble ahead,' he said to Finn, lowering the binoculars, fear widening his small eyes. 'Serious trouble. We've got twenty minutes to batten down the hatches.' He raised the binoculars once more to his eyes, adding, 'And then we're in the hands of the gods.'

CHAPTER THIRTY

Sabotage Part 2

NORWAY 1944

Hans had had a growing sense of anticipation that something was about to happen. All had been too quiet since the last attempt on *Tirpitz* and, with winter around the corner, the opportunity to strike was closing fast. The night had been clear and bright: perfect conditions for a bombing expedition. Hans was tossing and turning restlessly in bed when a shower of grit was thrown at his window.

He bolted out of bed and, sweeping the curtain aside, he pressed his face against the glass, cupping his eyes so he could peer into the darkness. As he expected, Erik's outline hovered outside his window. He gave him a thumbs up, hoping that Erik would be able to see, and then he swiftly got dressed. He crept out of his hut and into the night. Erik stood directly beside the door. He pulled Hans's arm and the two walked silently out along the path.

'I have urgent news from the agent,' whispered Erik, when it was safe to do so. 'There's to be another attempt to bomb *Tirpitz* at around 8.30 this morning. There's so little time! What on earth can you do?'

Hans listened intently.

'It's what I don't do,' he murmured. 'The planes will be fast approaching the Norwegian coastline,' Hans continued. 'We have to find a way for me to man the radar station alone, Erik. We need to think of a diversion. But what?'

They stood in silence; Erik's mind raced.

'What about a fire?' suggested Erik. 'A fire, here at the huts?'

'In my hut,' said Hans, chewing over the idea. 'We can set a slow burner so that the fire takes hold well after we've gone. Then, when we are alerted at the radar station, I'll be able to send the others to deal with it while I man the station alone. That should give me enough time.'

'For what? I don't understand!' said Erik.

'The radar will alert me to the bombers as they fly into Norwegian airspace,' explained Hans. 'And at that point, I will do absolutely nothing.'

Erik understood. Sabotage on the highest level.

They turned and walked silently back to the huts. Once inside, Hans put on a low light in the kitchen area and rummaged around under a cupboard. He pulled out a box of candles and set one in a candlestick on the table. Then he left the room and returned with some sheets of paper.

'Tear these into long strips,' Hans said. Erik obliged and while he did this Hans went into his bedroom. When he reappeared, he carried a brown leather suitcase. 'Put the candle near the window,' he said to Erik.

A flimsy net curtain was pulled closed. Hans picked up some of the long strips of paper. Erik watched as he carefully twisted them and then wrapped them around the base of the candle. Then he continued the paper trail out along the table towards the curtain.

Erik could imagine the trail of the flickering flame from the melting candle down to the coils of paper. Here, burning and licking, it would thread along the paper to the curtain. The fire would take seconds to fly up the curtain and soon the wooden hut would be alight. It was so simple, and yet, so deadly.

'What if…' began Erik. 'What if the fire spreads into the other huts? What if someone gets hurt? There are men sleeping in these huts. We can't just let them burn!'

'We may be German, but that doesn't make us all Nazis. That's where you come in,' whispered Hans. 'I want you to hide in the bushes until you see smoke. Until the fire is climbing the curtains. Until you smell the faintest hint of burning.'

Erik listened carefully to his instructions.

'Then you shout and bang on the doors of the other huts.'

'What if I don't get the timing right?' said Erik.

'You will,' he said firmly. 'You say you're coming to tell me in the radar station. I can take it from there.'

'Won't they wonder what I'm doing here in the middle of the night?'

'They won't ask or think about it initially,' said Hans. 'You could always say later, if suspicion is aroused, that you were on one of your night time 'nature rambles', you know?' Hans shrugged. 'You can fill in the gaps. They're not important right now.'

Erik felt nerves and nausea pulsate through his veins.

Hans fetched the brown leather case.

'Take this when you leave and hide it somewhere nearby.

Somewhere safe.'

Erik grasped the case. His arm sank instantly with the weight.

'How will you explain that you managed to pack your things?' asked Erik.

'It's not what you think,' he smiled. 'But anyway, I'll not be staying around after this Erik.'

Erik swallowed. He still didn't quite understand how it was all going to work out. And how on earth was Hans able to simply disappear?

'Ready?' asked Hans.

Erik nodded. 'Ready,' he said.

Hans curled the corner of his mouth into a half-smile and patted Erik on the shoulder. He opened the door and Erik scuttled into the trees and the murky darkness clutching the case.

Hans turned back and looked round the hut one last time. Then he reached into his pocket and drew out a box of matches. He swiped a match until it glowed bright and then he carefully drew it to the candle wick. He watched it burn innocently, gently flickering in the breeze. Then he turned and walked out, carefully closing the door behind him.

CHAPTER THIRTY-ONE

Sabotage Part 3

NORWAY 1944

Erik hauled the heavy suitcase further into the woodland and found a stump to perch on. Through the branches, he could just make out the window of the hut. He stared hard into the darkness until the shapes before him seemed to dance and jump in front of his eyes. The animals moved and rustled in the forest behind him. The odd cackle and call of seabirds broke the silence and the gentle lapping of the sea was rhythmically reassuring. After a few minutes, distant footsteps made his heart run cold. But then he remembered it was Hans heading off up the path to the radar station.

Erik hid the suitcase under some branches nearby, grateful to be rid of it, and mentally tried to memorise its location. This was it. Attempting to focus his senses, Erik momentarily closed his eyes, carefully scrutinising every sound. Then, he took a deep lungful of freezing air, expecting at any second to catch a whiff of burning wood. How long would that candle take to burn down? Did they have time for all this waiting around? It was well after six o'clock now. Wouldn't the bombers be halfway here?

Nervous energy had kept him warm throughout the

night's adventures so far, but this was beginning to subside. He felt himself trembling and shivering with cold—it was freezing, after all. His jaw rattled uncontrollably and his arms ached from hauling that ridiculous case. Looking down, he checked again that as much greenery as possible was covering the sheen of the brown leather, but it was hard to see in the dark. All he could do was hope he could find it again in the daylight. Everything might look very different then.

When he glanced back up, in the glow of the light, the net curtains on the window seemed to be shrinking before his eyes. He gave his glasses a quick rub with his fingers. Was this it? Could he trust what he was seeing? Once again he filled his lungs. He held his nose for a second and did it again. There it was—the unmistakable aroma of burning. Without waiting another second he shot through the bushes, scrambling and tripping as he went. Acrid fumes hit him and a flickering bright orange light seeped through the branches ahead of him. The air was no longer clear and crisp but thick, smoky and cloying. How quickly the fire had taken!

By the light of Hans's hut now ablaze, Erik could clearly see the entrances to the two other huts that stood alongside it. He ran, shouting and screaming, slamming his hand on the windows. Erik burst through the door, turning immediately into the side room that was the bedroom. Two men lay sound asleep in their metal-framed beds. Erik shook the one nearest him.

'Fire! Fire!' he screamed.

The man stirred and blinked at Erik in confusion. But

then he seemed to understand. He leapt up and grabbed his colleague in the other bed and they dashed outside.

The two men ran to the last hut and awoke their colleague who was also sound asleep inside. They all stood staring at the fire in horror.

The men bolted back inside to grab as many of their belongings as they could. They shouted urgently to each other in German and, once outside, set about gathering buckets from the outhouse. Erik saw his chance.

'I'll go and tell Hans!' shouted Erik to the men when they reappeared. They nodded.

'Tell Hans his hut is gone. There is nothing left!' called a German. 'We need help to save the rest of the billets.'

Erik took off. His legs pounded as fast as they would go along the narrow path, the branches of trees and shrubs grabbing at his shins. Erik made it up onto the road and then belted towards Seal Point and the radar station. As soon as he reached the door, he forgot he was supposedly in role. There really was a fire causing devastation, after all. The fact that he had planned it was pushed to the back of his mind. He threw open the door and ran in. One of the other radar operators was inside making coffee; he looked up in surprise at the sight of Erik. Gasping for breath, Erik blurted out the words he had rehearsed in his head as he had run there.

'Fire! There's a fire at your billets. Where's Hans? Is he here?'

Hans appeared at the door from the radar machines.

'Erik?' he said, devoid of all emotion or intention.

'Your hut!' gasped Erik. 'It's burning. It's gone! A fire has ripped through it. The men are okay but they need help, otherwise their huts will be gone too!'

Hans made to grab his coat, but stopped abruptly and turned to his colleague who looked ashen. Another German had rushed through.

'You go, Kurt. And take Pieter too,' Hans said turning to the man behind them. 'I can stay here and man the fort alone. I can make a call to get help to you too.'

'Alone?' Kurt looked bewildered, shocked almost. 'Are you sure?'

Erik felt a rising sense of panic. Was he suspicious? He swallowed hard and shot a look to Hans who remained cool and unflinching.

'There's no time to discuss this. I know how to man the station alone. I've more experience than you both. Don't worry. I can keep things going for an hour or two; the chances of something significant happening in that time are slim. Now go!' he ordered.

They paused, looking at each other, then Hans. Erik blinked slowly, feeling light-headed.

'Go!' Hans commanded again, raising his voice a little. His cheeks flared red ever so slightly.

Kurt nodded, sensing the rising urgency of the situation and, glancing nervously around, he grabbed his coat. Pieter did the same and then they turned and ran out the door. Hans and Erik watched them as they pelted up the hill towards the gate. Then Hans closed the door and looked at his watch. It was just after 7am. Finally, they were alone.

'It's already begun,' Hans said to Erik. 'The bombers have been spotted.'

Chapter Thirty-Two

Squall Line

The Norwegian Sea 2014

At first, Gus merely raised an eyebrow in doubt as he looked over at Finn. He was reclined in his seat in the wheelhouse with his feet up on the dashboard.

'Let me see,' Gus said doubtfully, peering through the binoculars. Olde sighed and clenched his jaw. The menacing streak on the horizon was now clearly visible without the binoculars. All at once, Gus's stubbornness seemed to drain away, along with the colour in his face.

'Oh man!' he grimaced looking out in the direction of the approaching storm. It was coming alright. 'How long have we got?' he asked Olde.

'I'd say less than twenty minutes,' Olde replied.

Finn bit his lip. But then he couldn't contain himself any longer. Something made him snap, 'You idiot, Gus! Check you out, just sitting there, feet up like you're on flippin' *Deadliest Catch!*'

Gus's eyes flashed in disbelief and anger.

'What the hell do you know, anyway?' Finn's rant continued, froth flecking from his lips. 'Not much more than me, I reckon! You should've listened to Olde, you complete tool! Now we might turn turtle thanks to you!' And, realising the implications of what he'd said, he added, now yelling, 'We might *die* Gus!'

Gus looked at his little brother in horror. He lunged towards him in rage and grabbed his sweater at the neck.

'Don't talk to me like that you little...' he stopped himself. Then, regaining composure, he said, 'I'm your skipper, remember. Do you hear me? Talk to me like that again and I'll...'

'What? Make me walk the plank?' interjected Finn.

'Boys!' Olde barked at his two great-grandsons. 'We're wasting precious time. Look!'

Sure enough, the dark clouds were drawing closer.

'If it moves, it needs to be tied down,' Olde stated, taking control. 'We're in for a hell of a ride.'

Gus didn't wait to be told twice. He pushed past his brother and set to work. They took Olde at his word and secured *The Northern Light*. Every crank, tool, crane, fish box and coffee cup was tied down or stashed into a cupboard. Olde too was tied into a seat in the wheelhouse and, as the waves began to roll, they were as ready as they'd ever be.

'You've been through one of these before haven't you, Olde?' said Finn, fear creeping into his voice. 'And it'll be okay?'

He smiled at the old man, looking for reassurance. Even just a shred of hope that somehow this wasn't a huge deal and that later on they would laugh at the whole experience. Because under the surface, Finn was terrified. The malevolent line of clouds was fast approaching. He imagined their small vessel being tossed around like a paper boat until overcome by the tipping, rolling waves. To be swallowed up by the ocean; it was Finn's worst nightmare. He looked towards Olde, searching for a fragment of hope.

Olde looked wistfully out the window. His fingers drummed softly on the dashboard. Until finally he spoke, his voice steady and calm.

'I've been through a few bad ones,' he conceded. He paused and then added, 'One was particularly memorable.'

'Well, you're still here to tell the tale,' said Gus, breaking the silence. 'Right, Olde?'

Finn glanced over at his brother who was clearly trying to gain one up on him and felt another surge of annoyance. He'd never experienced this level of tension towards Gus. It was unsettling.

Olde nodded. 'Yes, Gus, I'm still here alright. We'll be fine, boys,' he said, reaching out his arms. He laid a hand on Gus's shoulder and the other on Finn.

'Worse things have happened at sea,' he said quietly. 'We'll get through this. One way or another. Try to steer head on, Gus. We don't want any rogue waves over the broadside.'

Gus nodded and focused ahead, his face fixed in a steely determination.

The wind whipped up now and the boat rolled more violently. It wasn't long before the full force of the storm was upon them. Wave after wave lined up to have a go at tipping them. Like a roller coaster, they were lifted up to be thrown down. Water smashed against the window. The wind screamed and the rain pelted against them like buckets of gravel. They gripped whatever they could, their knuckles white, bracing themselves every time a wave hit. Finn closed his eyes and tried to block out the terror, nausea and violent rocking. Suddenly, Gus yelled out above the shriek of the wind, 'Something's wrong! Olde! Finn!'

Finn could barely hear him above the chaos but he could see his face drained of all colour.

'It's the steering!' Gus bellowed. 'The steering's gone! I've no control!'

CHAPTER THIRTY-THREE

Tirpitz Day

NOVEMBER 12TH, NORWAY 1944

Several hundred miles away from Tromsø, flying below the radar at just under two-thousand feet, twenty-nine Lancaster Bombers crossed into Norwegian airspace. They had left Scotland in the early hours, and now each member of the crew sat tense and focused. Their mission was simple: get the beast once and for all: decimate *Tirpitz*.

Achieving this had been pummelled into them—like the fist of Churchill slamming down on his polished desk in the cabinet war office. They must succeed, even if it meant sacrificing their own lives. It was, quite simply, their duty.

Their planes had been stripped out to make way for the massive Tall Boy bombs. The smell from the extra tanks of fuel stacked up for their long flight was intense. The crew tried to ignore its potent pungency, but still it made them nauseous. They were anxious. Anxious to get the job done, but also because they knew that the Germans would be ready with their fighter planes to defend their famous warship. They would be scrutinising their radar and, in minutes from being sighted, they could be shot out of the sky, shattered into a thousand pieces.

The skies were beautifully clear as they began to climb steadily. They would have no problem finding their target. But neither would the German fighter planes. The crew didn't dwell. Now was the time. The Wing Commander checked his watch. It was 7.40am exactly. The bombers crossed into Sweden and came together, changing direction. It was time to head north.

Erik checked his watch. Forty minutes had passed since Hans had been contacted by another coastal radar station about possible sightings of the bombers on the coast of Norway. He'd tried to throw them off the scent by making suggestions that the planes were en route to Russia.

Erik looked out once again towards the gate. All was quiet. Unable to remain still, he closed the door and shuffled into the control room. Hans was staring intensely at the small screen that wavered in front of him. Every so often, he tinkered with the knobs on the control panel.

'Any minute now my screen will pick up the bombers,' Hans muttered. A tense silence hung between them. The shrill ring of the telephone beside Hans shattered the stillness. Hans snatched it up. Erik listened as he spoke calmly in German and placed the phone down.

'*Tirpitz*,' he said. 'They're receiving confused sightings.'

Erik stood, his heart thumping in his throat as he hovered at the door. He needed to make sure that no one was heading down their way, but he became aware of the sound of beeps and many small dots creeping in to Hans's screen, lit up by the rotating line.

'What's that? Is that them?' he whispered, unable to tear

his eyes away.

Hans nodded. 'They're coming.'

Erik swallowed hard.

'What do we do now?' he said, trying to mask his rising panic.

Hans turned to look at him. His face serious and intense. 'Erik. We do nothing. We do nothing.'

For those ten minutes that passed, Erik felt a strange mix of melancholy and impending doom. Not for themselves, but for the hundreds of lives that were about to be lost aboard *Tirpitz*—the ordinary German sailors who were going about their duties. Erik sensed that Hans felt the same.

'Hans,' Erik said, breaking the silence. 'Are you sure? You said yourself, being German doesn't make you a Nazi. Those sailors...' Erik stopped himself from saying anymore.

Hans bowed his head but said nothing.

The telephone rang again, it seemed deafening this time. They both jumped.

Hans lifted the receiver and spoke quietly. He shook his head as he spoke and replaced the receiver softly.

'*Tirpitz* again. They have confirmed sightings, thirty minutes away. They don't understand why I haven't picked up any readings.'

He waited a little longer, every so often glancing at his watch. Then he picked up the phone and spoke quickly in German.

'I have alerted the air base at Bardufoss,' said Hans calmly. 'I've given them incorrect readings. I have told them they are forty minutes away. They wanted to know if an incoming Junker could land. I said, based on my readings, they had plenty of time. That should delay their fighters by another five minutes. It's tight, but it should be okay.'

Hans stood and took a long breath.

'It's done. It's done,' he repeated, his back to Erik. 'We just have to hope and pray they hit their target.' He paused then spoke again, now staring at the screen in front of him. 'Sometimes, and it's regrettable, Erik, human sacrifice is required in order to slay the beast.'

Hans turned round slowly; his face was as white as the cigarette he had slipped into his mouth. Erik frowned. He realised that Hans wasn't looking at him. He was looking behind him at something else. Or someone else.

Erik swung round to see Kristoffer standing at the door of the radar station.

Chapter Thirty-Four

The Race

Norway 1944

Hans and Erik froze as they stared at Kristoffer's smug face.

'No, please,' he said, his blue eyes gleaming. 'That was just beginning to sound interesting. Do continue.'

Erik mentally retraced their conversation. How much had he heard? When had he come in? Had he seen the radar screen?

'Nice to see you again, Erik. I thought I might find you here. Where is everyone else?' Kristoffer looked around suspiciously. 'Surely you don't man this station by yourself?' He raised one eyebrow at Hans. 'You could get up to all sorts if no one else was around to keep an eye on you?'

Erik was dumbstruck, but Hans had managed to regain his composure, even coolly lighting his cigarette. But it was an interruption too far for Erik; he was burning with anxiety to know if, in fifteen minutes, the bombers would reach Tromsø and their floating target.

'I have no idea why you are here,' said Hans curtly, 'or who you think you are marching in here. Get out now, or I will have no option but to report you.'

'Oh yeah?' smirked Kristoffer. 'Report me to whom

exactly? My father is the police officer around here and happens to be tight with the Gestapo officers based in the village. You and Erik are up to something. I heard you talking. I'll make sure that it stops now whatever you...'

A fist boldly came into sharp contact with Kristoffer's jutting jaw. The blow was fierce and unforgiving. It threw him backwards and he fell to the floor heavily.

Erik shook the pain out of his right hand.

'Well done,' remarked Hans, looking down at Kristoffer, who was now out cold on the floor. 'No time to lose, Erik. Go to the village as fast as you can. Try to find Olsen. Tell him I need passage out of here as soon as possible. I had hoped I might be able to delay my departure a little to continue here. But Kristoffer knows too much. I have no choice.

'Then try to get to the far end of the island,' Hans continued. 'See what you can of *Tirpitz*. See if it has happened with your own eyes. I will wait at the cave for further instruction. *Our* cave.'

Erik nodded and quickly took off running towards the gate. He broke into a sprint; he had never felt his legs power him with quite such urgency. As he ran, Erik imagined the Lancasters, leaving the mountains of northern Sweden behind, circling in the milky light like great vultures. They would gather together, swarming into their killer formation, some higher than others, and on the signal they would commence their charge. Very soon *Tirpitz* would be in their sights.

Erik reached the school. It was locked. He rattled the door needlessly. Of course, there was no school today.

Olsen was nowhere to be seen. He must be away in another village. Erik ran to the shop and burst in. Per Johansen was talking quietly to a customer and both looked startled at the sight of Erik, sweating and panting at the door. Per was quick to cover him.

'Ah Erik! You're here at last. I have your parents' order for you,' he improvised. 'Go round the back, I'll only be a minute,' he said briskly.

Erik grimaced and scuttled through. Magnus was in the kitchen eating his breakfast. Per, having got rid of his customer, rushed through quickly.

'*Tirpitz* is to be bombed any minute,' Erik gasped. 'Hans needs passage out, Mr. Johansen. I need to find Mr. Olsen.'

Per nodded slowly, absorbing the information.

'I have to go now to see if *Tirpitz* has been hit,' continued Erik breathlessly.

Magnus jumped up, his mouth still full of porridge.

'I'm coming too.'

Erik looked at Per. 'Can you help? Can we get Hans out?'

'I'm not sure what we can do,' he said. 'Olsen has left the village. I don't know when he'll be back. He could be miles away. I can't leave the shop; there are Germans everywhere.'

'He's in serious danger. Kristoffer knows,' warned Erik.

Deep horror and hatred flashed across Per's face. He pulled out a chair and sat down at the table, deep in thought.

'Your father, Erik. He's our only hope,' he said earnestly.

Erik felt a stab of panic and confusion. 'My *father*? What can he do?'

'He's a fisherman—he has a boat! He can get Hans away and hopefully meet up with the Shetland boats—the bus they call it—to give him safe passage to Scotland.'

'It's too dangerous!' Erik tried to control his emotions. 'There will be patrol boats on the fjord! They'll stop and search him. They'll know!'

Per shook his head. His face despondent. There was nothing else he could suggest.

Magnus grabbed Erik's arm.

'We need to go. Now!' shouted Magnus, snatching up a pair of binoculars. 'Where's your bike, Erik?'

Erik tore himself away from Per and the two boys ran to the village hall to retrieve the bike. With Magnus behind him, Erik pedalled as if his life depended on it and they sped up onto the road, leaving the village far behind, heading up the fjord. Soon, they became aware of distant, rapid bursts, like small explosions. The flak guns had started up: the Lancasters had arrived. That was a sign, surely: a good sign. The German bombers hadn't got them; Hans's plan must have worked!

As Erik pedalled, an almighty judder vibrated beneath them; even though they were expecting it, hoping for it, when it came, it was sudden and violent. The scream and boom of each Tall Boy bomb ripped and reverberated up and down the fjord with terrifying force. The impact tore through the air around them, rippling through their veins, shaking every molecule of their bodies. They gripped hard, scared they would be thrown to the ground. Magnus shrieked with excitement in Erik's ear.

The power and the noise, and the satisfaction that the symbol of their country's oppression was being attacked, was both petrifying and thrilling at the same time. With each thunderous explosion, images flashed through Erik's mind: images of horrors and destruction, but also of victory.

The pounding continued as they sped around the corner, giving them a clear view up the fjord towards Håkøya island and the position of *Tirpitz's* resting place. They leapt off the bike and onto the grass panting from terrified exhaustion.

'Look!' yelled Magnus, pointing upwards.

High above them, a cluster of black dots swarmed across the crystal clear sky; the Lancasters were departing. It was all over so quickly—it could only have lasted a matter of minutes. Ahead of them, smoke blocked any view of the battleship and they had to pedal further round the island for a better look.

The bike stopped again and they squinted out over the water.

'Well?' shouted Erik. 'Has she been hit?'

Magnus peered through his binoculars and smiled, passing them over to Erik.

As the smoke gradually shifted, the outline was blurry but unmistakable. *Tirpitz*, "the beast", was on her side.

Chapter Thirty-Five

Struggles at Sea, Part 1
The Norwegian Sea 2014

Gus had never seen the sea look so big, so intense and terrifying; each swell seemed mightier and angrier than the last. And now they were drifting, unable to steer, swirling at the mercy of the waves. One rogue wave and *The Northern Light* would be swamped. Fear sat tight in Gus's throat. He looked over to Olde, who seemed remarkably calm and focused.

'I'll take over here,' Olde shouted over the noise to Gus. 'You go below to the engine room, see what's going on.' Then he added, 'We're not done for yet! Get down there, Skipper. You'll get to the bottom of this.'

Gus nodded and battling against the violent sways of the boat, slipped down to the engine room below. 'Finn, you go between us—then I can hear what's going on!'

Finn nodded, clearly relieved to be given direction.

Gus battled doubt as he frantically started to look around. Perhaps Finn was right. Perhaps he really wasn't up to attempting this. He wondered if he really did know how to skipper a boat. When it had come to fixing problems in the engine room, he'd always left that to his father. He tried to think methodically. The engine thrummed rhythmically but as the boat lifted and dropped, like a heart missing a beat, the sound faltered, becoming stilted and staccato. It was struggling, Gus thought. He focussed hard and noticed that something was leaking; there was oil everywhere.

'Something's leaking!' Gus yelled up to Finn, who was staring down, looking as though he were about to vomit.

Gus heard Finn update Olde. Then he vaguely heard Olde's voice over the wind howling outside.

'Hydraulic fluid,' Finn yelled repeating Olde's words. 'Try and locate the leak!'

Gus nodded. It made sense. He began to feel as though he could sort this. He quickly found the steering pump, cleaned up the fluid and sure enough, the leak seemed be coming from the pressure gauge. He could fix this. They kept spares. Everything was going to be fine. He worked swiftly, focussing closely on the job in hand. Once the new pressure gauge was in place, he could see that the steering pump was up and running again.

'How's that?' he yelled up to Finn.

There was no reply.

Gus scrambled up the steps to the wheelhouse. Still the storm raged on, whipping rain and winds against the boat.

'How's that?' Gus shouted again to Olde, who was checking the steering now. He turned and gave a thumbs up.

'It's all back, Gus!' he said. 'Well done Skipper! The size of that rogue wave was monstrous,' remarked Olde. 'But this old girl is holding up well.' He patted the side of the dashboard. 'We'll be out the other side any minute.'

Gus looked around, the momentary thrill of having sorted the problem below deck like a true pro and surviving a rogue wave, had now drained from him.

'Where's Finn?' he asked. Even saying those two words ignited a new level of truly horrifying fear.

Olde spun his head round with a look of horror. 'I thought he was below with you!'

Gus felt his heart pound. He didn't bother going back down below to check. He knew he wouldn't be there. Somehow he just knew he had gone out on deck, and was in trouble.

He battled his way outside. The winds were horrendous. He was thrown around like a rag doll, unable to direct his own simple movement of walking a matter of yards. Despite their best efforts at securing everything, boxes and cables seemed to be swinging around. With each tip of the boat, the sea appeared beside him, pawing at him with spray. A stagger too far and he would be overboard. He frantically looked around.

'Finn!' he shrieked desperately over the roar of the storm. 'Finn!' he could feel his voice breaking. He felt sick—gripped by a desperate fear that his brother had gone overboard. And then he noticed something. The massive net that they used to trawl for prawns had partially unspooled and was trailing over the side. Lurching across the deck, Gus realised in horror that he could see what appeared to be a foot. He leaned over the edge, dreading that his nightmare would be confirmed—sure enough, the foot was attached to Finn, upside down, his face towards the ocean. The waves crashed and pulled at him. His body was cocooned in the twisted net and he was dangling precariously—completely helpless like a fly on a web.

Gus tried reaching down to grab his brother, but he was terrified that the wrong move could send him into the sea. He tried to wind the net back in but it was jammed and wouldn't budge.

He shouted and called to his brother. No response. Gus panicked. Was he already dead? Had he somehow been submerged and drowned? Gus quickly pushed that notion out of his head. There was nothing for it. He would have to pull him up by his legs. All the while the boat slammed into the waves. Gus leaned over and grabbed his brother with all his might. Somewhere above Gus's head a thick metal cable had become loose and thwacked him with terrible force across his back. He twisted his head around and ducked just in time as it swung back from the crane above. He grabbed at Finn's legs, dodging the cable that could, at any moment, at best render him unconscious, at worst, throw him into the waves. He leaned over, now perilously close to losing his balance, and he reached again for his brother's foot, or leg, or anything that he could hold onto firmly. It was no use. Something was stopping his brother from shifting. He was tangled tightly into the net.

As the storm raged around him, Gus despaired. He couldn't ask Olde for help and he couldn't leave his brother. He had only one option left. He reached for the knife on his belt.

He would have to cut the net.

CHAPTER THIRTY-SIX

Hans on the Run

NORWAY 1944

Hans sat in the still of the gloomy cave. He was convinced he'd managed to remain unseen, journeying from the radar station to the cave, and now there was nothing more he could do but wait. The cave was damp; his breath blew white in the freezing air. What he was waiting for exactly, he didn't know. He'd put his life in the hands of Erik. He stood and paced the cave, pondering that very reality: his life in the hands of a teenage boy.

He stopped. All his senses were on high alert. There was a change. Something or someone was approaching. Hans edged carefully to the mouth of the cave and tried to quieten his own breathing so as to assess the sounds all around. He clearly heard distant branches snapping, feet traipsing through the undergrowth. Was it Erik? He couldn't be sure. It sounded like more than one person. Possibly many people. Then his blood ran cold. Someone out there, cursed. The voice was still far away, but distinctive nonetheless.

'Damn!' said the voice sharply, as if he'd tripped or caught his foot.

'Be quiet, boy!'

Hans knew who it was: Kristoffer and his treacherous quisling father.

Wasting no time, Hans pulled off his shoes and crept out of the cave before they came too close. He crouched low so that they wouldn't see him. Hans was trapped. He couldn't go back up the hill as he would meet them head on, and if he waited in the cave he would be discovered. He had no choice. He waded into the freezing water clutching his shoes—he could leave no clue. The bitter temperature of the water momentarily took his breath away. The depth soon dropped sharply, dragging and pulling his thick woollen sweater. Hugging close to the caves and rocks of the coast, Hans began to swim. As soon as it was safe, he moved to the side and clutched to a break in the rocks. He stuffed his shoes into a crack. In the distance, there were men shouting. Hans clung on and strained to hear what was being said, his body now shuddering in the icy water. He tried to keep moving.

'No! Not here,' called a voice.

'There's no sign of him!'

'Are you sure *this* was the cave? There are many nearer the radar station, round at Seal Point.'

'Yes, father!' implored the whiny voice of Kristoffer. 'I saw him here with Erik. I'm sure. I'm sure this is the cave he meant. I heard him tell Erik after the rat punched me,' he spat angrily.

'Well, there's no sign of him now and nowhere to hide,' his father snapped. 'Try the caves further round.'

The footsteps crunched on the pebble beach and then back up through the foliage. It sounded as though several

Nazi henchmen were out searching for him.

Hans didn't wait. This had bought him some time. There were no caves between here and where he pictured Erik's house to be, so they would be heading in the other direction —it might keep them busy while he made his way further up the fjord. He had to get moving before his body froze. And so now he swam and sometimes waded, cautiously, all the time staying as close to the shore as possible, but not so close that he could be seen. He felt himself begin to slow. He was getting tired and his limbs were heavy and numb. The cold penetrated his mind now. He was overwhelmed. Sleep was near.

A new sound caught his attention and snapped him out of his crushing exhaustion. Adrenalin coursed through his veins. A boat was coming up the fjord. He edged himself to the rocks and awkwardly twisted his head. It was as he feared. A German patrol boat sliced through the water, heading towards him at a fair pace. He was at the narrowest part of the fjord and he would be seen unless he concealed himself quickly. Hans hauled himself onto a ledge. It was narrow and, now out of the water, his body trembled with cold. All the time, the engine of the patrol boat became louder. With his shaking fingers, Hans pulled himself along the ledge. He could feel his heart pumping; his throat pulsated with its beat. He could see a break in the ledge where he could crouch. With only seconds to spare until he would be in sight, Hans swung himself into the gap in the rock and pressed his body as small as he possibly could. The roar of the boat engine intensified as it approached, echoing around the narrow section of the fjord.

Hans's body rattled against the stone, his teeth chattered. The boat was now level with him and if the Nazis were using binoculars they would have spotted his shape, crushed against the rock. Hans braced himself.

Perhaps they would fire a shot. Perhaps it would all be over.

But the boat didn't falter. It didn't slow or stop. The hum of the engine quietened as the boat continued its journey, sweeping towards Tromsø. Towards *Tirpitz*. Or what was left of her, Hans mused. That's why they weren't looking for him. They were needed elsewhere.

He didn't have time to let his mind wander to the horrors they might find, as the ledge he was teetering on crumbled. Despite desperate scrambling, it gave way and he fell, crashing into the water below, smashing his arm, bone on rock, as he dropped.

Chapter Thirty-Seven

Struggles at Sea, Part 2
The Norwegian Sea 2014

Gus pulled out his rescue knife, and clutching Finn's leg with one hand, he leaned awkwardly over and began to saw through the net. At first the waves continued to pound the side of the boat, soaking him as he tried to free his brother. But then he could sense that Olde was now able to steer into the oncoming storm.

With one slice, he could feel his brother's body weight shift in the tangled net. If he cut too much, he would simply allow his brother to slip into the torrent below. And Finn would be gone. He leaned down and, with all the strength he could muster, hauled. He could feel Finn beginning to move. The boat continued to tip and pull in the storm and he tried desperately to keep his balance as he was thrown from side to side. A stumble too far and he too would be overboard, and Olde would have no idea that his two great-grandsons were gone.

His fingers grasped and pulled. Very slowly, he managed to drag Finn back up. One final cut and he would fall the right side of the hull. He sawed frantically at the tangled section of net, until Finn's weight finally slumped onto the deck with a heavy thud.

'Finn!' he yelled. 'Finn!'

Gus knelt down and shook his brother's shoulders. His face was pale; his eyes were closed. There was no sign of life.

Panicking, Gus stared desperately into Finn's face. There was a flicker in his cheek and a soft moan. Finn was stirring! He opened his eyes and promptly rolled over and threw up.

Gus breathed out heavily in utter relief and put a hand on his brother's back as he vomited once more over the deck.

'You had me worried there, mate,' he said. 'That was about as close as it gets.'

Gus shook his head. The severity of what had just happened was now sinking in. He sat down heavily on the deck floor and wiped his brow.

Finn, now shivering, wrapped his arms around himself and rubbed his limbs. He turned and looked at his brother and gave a small smile, only slightly turning the corners of his mouth.

'Thanks,' he murmured. Then his smiled dropped and a look of shock crossed over his face. 'What the...?' he gasped through his shivers. 'Oh no, Dad's gonna kill you!'

Gus followed his line of vision to the cut net spilling out into the jaws of the sea.

'You cut the net?' said Finn, with a look of disgust.

Gus shook his head and rolled his eyes. He shook his fist playfully at his brother.

'Aye. And it's coming out of your wages, ya wee git,' he said. He was about to launch into a tirade about Finn coming out on deck by himself in the storm, but his brother's voice interrupted his thoughts.

'The storm!' he said.

Gus looked up. With all the commotion he hadn't noticed. The storm had passed. A calm had descended upon them and blue sky had opened up above.

The door to the wheelhouse swung open and Olde came staggering out, his face tense and pensive.

'Everything okay out here?' he said. 'Finn—you're soaking! Been for a swim, boy?'

'Aye, I mean no, Olde,' said Finn, still chattering. He shook his head. 'We're out the other side, eh?'

They all stood now and gazed out over the calm sea. No one said a word, until Finn broke the silence,

'Look!' he shouted, pointing to snow-capped mountains in the distance.

'Ah yes!' Olde nodded. 'The Lofoten Islands! Boys— welcome to Norway!'

'How does it feel, Olde?' said Gus. 'To be coming home, after all this time? You've not been back since the war, right?'

Olde was quiet. He stared out towards the majestic mountains that stretched from the sea to the clouds.

'Ah, well,' he murmured. Then he turned to face his two great-grandsons. 'Norway is not my homeland,' he said quietly. He seemed to be searching their faces for a reaction to this simple statement.

'I know Shetland is your home,' said Gus. 'What I meant, is you're returning to the place you were born and raised. Your nation!'

'I know what you meant,' said Olde. 'I suppose I'm an honorary Norwegian, but I wasn't born here. And I wasn't raised here.'

Gus and Finn looked perplexed.

'I was posted here during the war as a radar operator. Working for the Nazis.' Olde cleared his throat. 'You see, boys, I'm German. My real name is Hans.'

Chapter Thirty-Eight

Erik's Father

Norway 1944

Erik's father shook his head and turned to look out of the window, placing his pipe firmly back in his mouth.

'Please, father!' Erik begged. 'You have to believe me! If it wasn't for Hans, *Tirpitz* would still be sitting there!'

'I'm not helping a *Nazi*, Erik,' he hissed angrily, snatching the pipe out of his mouth. 'That's what you're asking me to do! Do you know what people would think of me? Of us in this community, if it gets out I helped a Nazi escape?'

Erik's face was blotchy and red.

'He's not a Nazi,' said Erik quietly.

'I didn't believe it either, sir!' blurted Magnus, who had been standing loyally at Erik's side. 'But it's true! He helped my father! The Resistance *know* him. He's on our side!'

Erik's father swung round and glared at the two boys.

'You two are naive if you believe that!'

'I'll go now and fetch father!' said Magnus.

Erik looked despondent. 'There's no time!' he wailed. 'Hans is waiting for help. Right now.' He pleaded once more with his father adding, 'Help from *us*! We're his only hope!'

But his father's silence meant his mind was made up.

Just then, they were interrupted by loud thumping on the door. A fist beating on wood.

'Open up! It's the police!' shouted an angry voice.

It was Kristoffer's father.

Erik and Magnus froze, their eyes wide. They glanced at each other, terrified. The banging started again. This time more forcefully.

Erik's father lifted a finger to his lips in a gesture to the two boys and calmly went to open the door.

Kristoffer's father strode in without being asked, followed by his son, a Gestapo officer, and two Nazi uniformed soldiers who immediately began poking around the room. And then without invitation they thundered heavily up the wooden stairs.

Erik's father stood with his back to the wall and folded his arms. He said nothing as they searched the house. His face was grim and defiant.

The police chief smirked and marched over to him. Kristoffer stood beside his father in the same wide-legged pose, but directed his stare at Erik.

'Your boy's been up to no good,' the police chief said.

Erik could feel his cheeks burn.

'Been helping some German turn-coat,' he added, 'blow up the Führer's warship.'

Erik stared down at the floor.

'Your little plan to meet him in that cave didn't work, eh Erik? Thought I hadn't heard you, eh? And now he's on the run,' burst out Kristoffer.

His father swiftly cut him off, throwing Kristoffer a warning glance. 'We'll find him,' he continued, his voice now a little shrill. 'Then hand him over. Do you know what the Führer does to traitors?' His eyes were darting excitedly.

Erik glanced over to the Gestapo officer. His face seemed to twitch, his fingers tapping impatiently on the folds of his shiny leather trench coat.

'And you'll pay too. D'you hear that, Erik?' The police chief's rant continued, flecks of saliva building into a sticky froth on his lips. 'You and your father will pay. You'll both take a little trip to the concentration camps in Poland.'

He then turned his venom on Magnus.

'And you and Per. Don't think we don't know that you're up to your necks in this too.'

A silence fell across the room broken only by the sound of the soldiers' heavy footsteps upstairs.

'And what if you don't find him?' Erik's father spoke, defiantly.

The police chief let out a low, malevolent laugh. 'Oh, we'll find him,' he replied. 'We'll hunt him down, even if it takes a lifetime.'

The two soldiers reappeared and shook their heads.

The Gestapo officer sucked in his cheeks and muttered something to them in German. Kristoffer's father was about to continue talking when he was sharply interrupted.

'This is a waste of time,' the Gestapo officer spat, retrieving a pair of gloves from the pockets of this trench coat. 'We have more important priorities,' he added, carefully and precisely pulling each finger into its leathered position.

The police chief reddened, his jaw tight.

'But he helped him!' Kristoffer protested. 'I heard them! I saw them! They're going to try to help that German! He's a traitor!'

'Silence, boy!' the Gestapo officer barked. Kristoffer's face fell. His father glared.

'There is nothing in this shack,' added the officer, looking around with disdain. 'This is nothing more than a wild goose chase and a waste of our time!'

He turned to leave, the two soldiers following smartly behind.

Kristoffer and his father both lingered, anger and humiliation brimming in their faces.

'This isn't over,' the police chief threatened as they turned to leave. He signalled sharply to his son to move.

'The war is almost over!' Erik's father spoke clearly, as they approached the door. 'And what will you do then, Alek?' Hearing his first name made Kristoffer's father flinch. He stopped still. But Erik's father continued. 'I've known you, man and boy. When the Nazis run, will you stay here and face your fellow Norwegians?' he paused. 'Or will you run with them like a pack of wolves, your tail between your legs?'

The police chief said nothing. He didn't move. Then with one swift action, he turned his head and spat on the kitchen floor. Without looking back, he marched out, leaving the door swinging on its hinges.

Erik's father calmly walked over and shut the door quietly. He turned to Erik and Magnus and said, 'Come on, boys, let's take a trip on the boat. I think we have some fishing to do. Fishing for a German hero!'

Erik clenched his eyes shut gratefully. When suddenly they heard a thud outside the back of the house.

'What are they up to now?' growled Erik's father, flinging open the back door.

Standing in the doorway was Hans. He was bloodied and limp.

'Have they gone?' he stammered in Norwegian, and collapsed heavily on the floor in front of them.

CHAPTER THIRTY-NINE

Farewell

NORWAY 1944

His arm was broken. He was covered in cuts and bruises, but all Hans wanted to know, when he was conscious once more, was whether they had done it—whether they had created enough time and space for the bombers to get to *Tirpitz*.

'We saw her with our own eyes,' said Erik. 'Through the smoke, we could see she had overturned.'

'We even spotted the bombers as they flew overhead,' added Magnus.

Hans's eyes were wide. He slowly absorbed the information. Erik's mother had arrived home now and, after a detailed explanation, was busy cleaning his wounds. She eyed her patient warily.

'Was *Tirpitz* on her side?' Hans asked, creating a mental picture in his head. His mind was swimming.

The boys nodded.

Hans was quiet. The colour had drained from his face; he felt faint. Was it the excruciating pain in his arm? Or was it the thought of his fellow Germans dying? He took a deep breath and tried to regain a sense of perspective.

'They say many men are trapped. Drowning,' said Erik's mother, now binding Hans's arm. 'Everyone's whispering about it in the village.' She paused and then added, 'They say the bombs came down so fast that they didn't stand a chance. No time to even catch their breath.' She shook her head.

She took a long piece of cloth and deftly created a sling for Hans's arm. She reached into a cupboard and fumbled at the back for a small bottle, which she uncorked and poured some liquid into a glass.

'Drink this,' she instructed Hans. 'It's medicinal.'

Hans took a sip. It was sharp and potent and instantly soothing. It warmed his throat and sank to his stomach.

'Thanks,' he uttered, grateful for some comfort.

'There'll be patrol boats everywhere,' said Erik. 'How are we going to get Hans away from here? They'll be watching our every move. I wouldn't be surprised if that snake Kristoffer is out there, policing the fjord.'

'How did you manage to get here without being seen?' Magnus asked Hans.

'I saw the cars and managed to stay low down by the shore. I guessed they would search the house. They didn't think to check any further afield. When the car left, I managed to make it up to the door.'

'Kristoffer and his father would have searched outside, if they'd had the chance,' Erik's father said.

'I'm not sure the Gestapo suspect you, Hans,' said Erik.

'But they will when it's confirmed Hans has disappeared,' Erik's father interjected. 'The sooner we get you away from here, the better.'

'But to where?' added Magnus anxiously.

'I can sail you as far as Lofoten,' Erik's father said. He took his pipe out of his pocket and carefully filled it with tobacco. He shared a tense, momentary glance with his wife. Hans noticed. Had Erik's father been involved already? Then he cautiously opened his mouth to talk. 'I know of some fishermen there who have helped the Resistance,' he added. 'They could link up with the boats that go to Scotland. To Shetland. They call it the Shetland Bus.'

Hans nodded, now feeling a little revived. Spots of colour were returning to his cheeks. 'Yes, I've heard of that. It would be the best option. I don't fancy my chances trying to get to Sweden.'

Erik's father turned to his son and Magnus. 'Get word to Olsen as soon as you can that I'm taking Hans out to Lofoten. He'll radio the Resistance. They'll know to expect us.'

Erik stared at his father in awe.

His father noticed his son's shock. 'We all have to do our bit,' he said and lit his pipe.

Outside, darkness began to fall. A small rowing boat made its way along the fjord. Kristoffer, angry and bruised from his humiliation in Erik's kitchen, wasn't ready for defeat. He rested the oars momentarily and twisted his head awkwardly, scanning the water. He was searching for Erik's father's fishing boat. He spotted it rocking in its position near their croft. Spurred on, he started to row again, slicing the oars through the water. *Sabotage, eh Erik? Well, two can play at that game.*

Back inside the farmhouse, Erik's father and Hans, now disguised as a fisherman, prepared to leave. They had packed food and supplies and stood awkwardly at the door.

'Goodbye, Erik,' said Hans. 'We made a good team, didn't we?' He reached out his good arm and they shook hands. Erik looked overcome with the realisation of what they had done; it fell between them as they said their goodbyes. Was it an achievement? Or something much darker? A frown burrowed into his forehead.

'We had to look at the bigger picture, Erik,' Hans read his mind. 'Never forget that. I will write to you once I've made it to Scotland.'

He shook hands with Magnus. 'Keep safe,' he said.

Hans struggled to pull a blue woollen hat down over his ears, his one hand reaching round both sides. Erik reached up to help. Hans smiled and, nodding to Erik's father, they turned and set off into the bitter darkness towards the water where the small fishing boat was moored.

'Hans!' blurted Erik urgently. He stopped and turned. 'Your suitcase—it's still buried near the radar station where I hid it!'

'Ah,' said Hans. 'Look after that for me,' he whispered. 'I'll come back for it—one day.'

He smiled again, reassuringly, his face pale and strained. Then turned and disappeared into the night.

And as an icy wind now began to whip and whistle, nobody heard the slap of oars on water as Kristoffer triumphantly rowed back down the fjord.

Chapter Forty

Welcoming Party
Norway 2014

'Olde? Or should we be calling you Hans? If, in fact that *is* your real name,' said Finn, with a glint in his eye as he brought another cup of black tea up the stairs.

Olde glanced over to Finn and smiled, reaching out to take his mug. 'Let's just stick with Olde, shall we?'

'Have you thought about what exactly we're going to do when we get there?' Finn continued.

'I've thought of little else since we set off,' said Olde, staring out at the coastline. There was a calmness about his surroundings, even though they were heading for the dangerous, the unknown. The sea was perfectly still, like a mirror, reflecting the mountains that sprung, lush and verdant out of the sea, piercing the clear blue sky like icy shards. Little wooden houses nestled along the coastline, and snow, sprinkled like a finishing touch of icing sugar, covered the mountainous peaks and pockets.

It was idyllic as far as the eye could see. But for Olde it sparked memories once again. Haunting and terrible memories of his escape from Norway all those years ago began to flood his mind: of that dark and bitterly cold night when they had said goodbye to Erik and Magnus; of the storm that had hit them; of losing Erik's father to the depths of the sea.

'I've been thinking about it too,' Gus chipped in, snapping Olde out of his dark thoughts. 'I think this really is a job for the police. With them having guns and stuff.'

Finn nodded in agreement.

'I mean, honestly Olde, what are we going to do?' he added, sounding increasingly nervous. 'These guys are properly, like, dangerous!'

Olde, Finn and Gus, all cramped together in the wheelhouse, eyed each other deep in thought.

'No,' said Olde firmly, pulling himself back to the present. 'It's me they want. Me alone. I intend to see this to the end. And you boys will have to trust me on this one.' He continued staring out at the sea and mountains beyond.

Finn and Gus threw each other a nervous glance.

'Well, according to the GPS, we're approaching the fjord for Tromsø. So this is it, I guess,' said Gus.

A tense knot now formed in Olde's stomach. He stood up and staggered out of the wheelhouse onto the deck and surveyed the coastline carefully with the binoculars. He could make out Seal Point where the radar station had been, and the caves along the coastline. Would he be able to spot the cave where he and Erik had discovered the gold? As their boat made its way along the fjord, he felt a strange sensation. Was it déjà vu? Or something else? A distant hum made him spin round and scan the fjord. Boats of all shapes and sizes were dotted along the water. But this particular noise became louder, echoing through the mountainous corridor. Then he spotted a small vessel powering some distance behind them.

Olde fumbled with the binoculars; it was a motorised dinghy of some description, whipping up white trails of foam. He could distinctly make out a tall man at the wheel. The man also had a pair of binoculars and looked directly back at him. Olde quickly snatched the binoculars away from his face, as if this would instantly make him invisible, and he bit his lip thinking through what was about to happen.

'This is just stunning,' said Finn, unaware and caught up in the beauty of the landscape.

'I think we have a welcoming party, boys,' Olde said.

Finn followed his line of vision.

'We're being followed?' he said.

'I think "escorted" might be the correct term,' said Olde, as the dinghy caught up with them. 'Good of them to come to meet us,' he added sarcastically.

Finn dashed into the wheelhouse to alert Gus as the large dinghy, drew up beside *The Northern Light*. Olde stayed outside standing defiantly. He recognised the Nazi they had met at Lerwick harbour.

'Follow on!' yelled the Nazi, over the noise of the engine, signalling with a flick of his chiselled chin. 'And no funny business this time!' He reached into his jacket, pulled out a gun and gestured with it that they should continue.

'What do we do now then?' muttered Finn, through his teeth, as if they could be heard as well as seen. 'I mean, what the hell are we gonna do?'

'We do as we are told,' murmured Olde, stumbling into the wheelhouse. 'For now,' he added.

All eyes were on the dinghy as it led them further and further up the fjord. Olde stared out the rain-speckled windows, across the landscape. His mind was searching, as were his eyes. Ahead was the rocky shore, but there were no distinguishing features. It was familiar, but it had been so long since his departure nothing seemed as it was.

As he turned his head, he noticed out of the corner of his eye, Finn fidgeting. He could tell he was uncomfortable—his jaw was clicking and he was grinding his teeth. He looked away, not wanting Finn to see his gaze, but Olde could tell he was up to something. In the reflection of the window, he could just make out Finn reaching for the rucksack. He was glancing around him now—he didn't want anyone to see. There was a flash of metal and Olde realised he had taken out the revolver.

Olde said nothing; he didn't want to draw attention to the lad, particularly with the Nazi watching their every move. Nor did he want Gus to know. It would only create a heated discussion. He could just make out Finn slipping the gun into his side pocket and fumbling with the zip. When it was done, he turned his head and gave Finn a wink.

'It's loaded,' he whispered. 'So be careful. You'll know when it's the right time to use it.'

Finn coloured a little that he'd been discovered. But then gave him a small thumbs up.

Their journey continued for some time, until they heard a shift in the engine ahead. They were slowing. Olde frowned, as they now veered over to the left of the fjord. A rickety wooden quay jutted some way out from the shore.

'It's never going to be deep enough to dock there!' said Gus, alarmed.

'It is. This fjord has surprising depths,' stated Olde. 'And there used to be a fishing boat here in my day.'

'So you know where we are?' said Finn.

'Yes,' said Olde, as if realising this for himself. 'They're not messing around. This was Erik's house.'

Chapter Forty-One

The Reunion

Norway 2014

'Tie up your boat,' yelled a voice from the quay. 'And we're watching your every move.'

The Nazi stood observing them carefully, then whipped out a phone from his back pocket and started talking hurriedly in Norwegian.

Gus directed *The Northern Light* alongside the dinghy, and with legs shaking Finn leapt out and secured the ropes.

'All of you off,' the Nazi barked. He stood overseeing them as they awkwardly helped Olde off the boat. It was the first time their feet had touched dry land in days. Olde felt a little disorientated.

'Up that way,' the Nazi ordered, and they set off walking away from the water. Finn and Gus took Olde's arms to help guide him along the path; the Nazi followed behind.

Panic gripped Olde momentarily that maybe Finn would be frisked for weapons. He glanced round at their captor. But the man clearly had little fear of his prisoners. Now they were here, on his turf, they were fully under his control.

'Move!' he ordered sharply. Olde swung his head back and followed on.

They all continued to walk, with a cautious eye on one another. It wasn't as Olde had remembered it. But then, he mused quietly to himself, it had been almost seventy years since that fateful day and indeed night, when he had run from the Nazis and from Norway itself. But as they approached the old farmhouse, something stirred in his memory. And with it came an overwhelming convulsion of guilt and horror—at what he had done—of all those who had died.

They were quickly ushered inside and into the kitchen. Olde looked around. The walls and ceilings were wooden-clad; frilled curtains framed the window. A large scrubbed table dominated the room. It would have been cosy, had it not been for the fact that they were being kidnapped.

They stood momentarily in silence, the Nazi guarding the back door, his face fixed to grim.

'Why are we here?' asked Olde. 'Where's Erik? I take it this is still his house?'

'And so, the traitor returns!' said a sneering voice interrupting the silence. Finn jumped. They all swung round to see an old man stagger into the kitchen from another door. He used a stick and was somewhat bent over, but clearly had once been a tall and impressive man. His fleshy limbs, once muscular and strong, now drooped, limp and saggy. His eyes were piercing blue, lighting up a craggy, yet handsome face. A thick mop of grey hair gave him a youthfulness, despite his elderly years.

'The one who got away, eh?' he continued shuffling forward, those blue, glassy eyes fixed closely on Olde.

Olde searched his face.

'The slayer of the beast! Destroyer of *Tirpitz*!' he announced dramatically, waving his stick.There she sat,' he now pointed vaguely in the direction of the fjord. 'And there she was hit! All thanks to this man here,' he paused, eyebrows raised, his arms wide in despair. 'That's right,' he continued. 'That beautiful creature was destroyed,' he said moving even closer to Olde, their faces almost touching, and then he spat the words, 'Destroyed! By a German!' His expression twisted his boyish features into something dark and sinister; now he was ugly. 'There the traitor cowers!' he declared, now standing back pointing a finger at Olde.

His voice was so loud and sharp that Finn and Gus both jumped. But Olde didn't flinch. He didn't say a word.

'And we thought you were dead!' The old man continued, sounding somewhat disappointed. 'Thought you'd been killed the night of your escape. When the boat sank and Erik's old man was drowned.' He turned and looked out the window, almost thinking out loud, 'Obviously, I didn't do my job properly that night. Allowing treacherous vermin like you to survive!' Olde frowned, trying to piece together what he was saying. Then the old man added, almost to himself, 'But I was so young then, and inexperienced in such things.'

'*You*,' said Olde quietly nodding. *Now* he realised who this bitter old man was. Of course. He shook his head in disbelief. After all these years. '*Kristoffer*,' Olde murmured.

The old man nodded with a smirk.

'So, Erik's father's fishing boat was meant to sink,' Olde said. 'You did something to the boat. So that the steering would fail.' Now it was making sense. 'Sabotage,' he hissed between his teeth.

Kristoffer smiled. 'Oh yes,' he conceded casually. 'On reflection,' he mused, 'I rushed it.'

Olde said nothing.

'I thought my job was done,' Kristoffer said. 'But, imagine my horror, my despair, when as chance would have it, I spotted you on television! Seventy years later!' He let out a chuckle.

They all looked at him blankly.

He continued, cheerfully, 'Yes, that's right. There you were! On my little television, sitting in the background, thinking no one would notice!' he continued. 'When our very own Norwegian Prime Minister opened that museum in Shetland. There you were—for all to see!

'At first,' he said, as if remembering a funny anecdote, 'At first I was angry. Furious even.' A broad smile grew across his face, revealing a row of white, pearly teeth. He raised a crooked finger into the air. 'But then my grandson Frederick here and I concocted a little plan.' He paused and shrugged his shoulders. 'I should be grateful, really. You gave me a new lease of life! Gave the *Werewolves* a new case!'

He moved close again to Olde, smiling. '*Now* is the time for revenge,' he said, his voice low and dark. 'It's never too late for revenge. Now *all* will hear the triumphant howl of The Werewolves! And what better timing!' he continued, his speech becoming more rousing, more dramatic. 'It will be seventy years this November since that terrible day. So now we can mark the anniversary of those needless and tragic deaths with *your* death!'

He seemed to drift into his own hazy daydream.

'*Tirpitz will* have her revenge at last,' he whispered. He looked around, his eyes sparkled; he was in his element.

'*Revenge*?' spat Olde, breaking this self-important silence. 'For what?' Your rantings are those of a lunatic! You have no idea what you're talking about!' Finn and Gus stared at their great-grandfather, who shouted with anger and disgust. His eyes flashed, his skin mottled and red.

Kristoffer swung round to face Olde.

'For betraying your fellow men!' he shouted. 'For your treachery. A thousand men died at your hands. And you thought you could just get away with it? I pieced together what I saw and what I heard that day in your radar hut,' he continued. 'You and Erik withheld vital information so that the fighters wouldn't have time to get to the British bombers. So that *Tirpitz* would be destroyed.'

Then with a sudden swift movement, Kristoffer thrust out a wrinkled hand and grabbed Olde by the throat. Finn and Gus gasped and moved to intervene, but they were stopped in their tracks by Frederick, who pulled them both back roughly

187

and held on to them with an iron grip.

'No, you slippery traitor!' shouted Kristoffer, still grasping Olde who was beginning to choke. 'You don't get away with betraying the Nazis. We never forget. And we will rise again. The Werewolves are building in strength and numbers all over Europe. Our acts of terrorism and extermination will raise our profile. And allow the world to see that The Third Reich will rise again!'

He released Olde, who instantly bent over coughing and wheezing.

Kristoffer seemed to take a breath, as though he were about to make a new announcement.

'And there's the little business of the *Tirpitz* gold,' he said boldly. 'I know that you and Erik know where it is. It is rightfully ours. It will be returned to us.' He stated this calmly, as though it were a matter of fact. 'It will fund further Werewolf "*activity*", shall we say.'

'Yours?' said Olde, incredulously, his voice strained and hoarse.

Kristoffer had said enough. He signalled to his grandson with a flick of his hand. Frederick leant down to the kitchen floor and lifted a rug. Underneath was the brass ring of a trap door. He lifted it and forcefully grabbed Gus and pushed him towards a narrow staircase that dropped below. Halfway down, Gus turned and aided Olde, who was being brusquely guided by Frederick. Finn came last.

When they were safely at the bottom they stared around, but it was too dark to see anything. The only light was from the kitchen above.

'You can enjoy a little reunion now,' Kristoffer said mockingly from the top of the staircase. 'I will return in an hour to be told where to find the gold. And if you defy me, you can expect to be shot.'

The trap door was dropped with a slam and the cellar was

plunged into the blackest darkness. Momentarily, there was silence; their shocked, frantic breathing was all that could be heard. But then another noise became apparent—muffled cries.

'What's that?' said Gus. 'Who's down here?'

Olde felt a grip of terror and reached for Gus's arm. There was a strike of a match which briefly lit up the corner and the outline of a man, bound and gagged, holding the tiny flame of light.

'Erik?' said Olde, straining to see.

The man nodded vigorously before the match burned out and they were once again in darkness.

Chapter Forty-Two

The Cellar

Norway 2014

'I have only a few matches left,' said Erik once they'd managed to pull off his gag. 'I've been down here for days, waiting for you to come.'

The second match now fizzled out. He struck one more and Gus fumbled to help Olde sit on a large storage box. 'Conserve the matches, Erik, my old friend' said Olde. 'We can talk in the darkness for a bit.'

'I can't believe; I mean I *didn't* believe it was possible,' Erik whispered. 'That you'd come,' he added. He reached out and took Olde's arm.

'When did this all begin, Erik?' asked Olde softly, signalling to Finn to help him sit down.

'Forever!' he said, with almost a laugh in his voice. 'Kristoffer and his family have been a tormenting presence here ever since the war. They were shunned and ostracised, but that hasn't deterred them—it has merely fed their bitterness. After his father's death, Kristoffer continued to poison his children's and grandchildren's minds with Nazi propaganda and ideals.' He paused and took a deep breath. 'But a few weeks ago things took a nasty turn. They barged their way into my house and have kept me prisoner, claiming that they were using me as human bait to lure in an old enemy. I had no idea that they meant you. They said that we would finally lead them to their "loot"—Kristoffer has never forgotten about the *Tirpitz* gold.

I've told them so many times where the gold was buried, even though you made me promise not to all those years ago.' He paused. Even in the dark, Olde could sense the guilt in his voice. 'I told them that Magnus and I saw the Nazis unload it into the cave and that we re-buried it there. I gave up trying to protect it—after their long running campaign of threats and abuse.'

'But they never found it,' said Olde, as more of a statement than a question.

'No,' said Erik. 'They have searched that cave—remember the one? The huge one, not far from where your hut was? They have been through it with metal detectors and specialised scanning equipment, but it has gone. I don't know where. Maybe the Nazis came back and retrieved it before they retreated out of Norway. Or some random gold digger discovered it years ago and kept it quiet. But the Werewolves are holding onto the belief that the *Tirpitz* gold is out there somewhere and it's tormenting them that they cannot find it,' Erik continued, his voice tired and broken. 'They've kept their true Nazi identity secret as they search. To the outside world it's a romantic hunt for buried treasure. For them it's crucial. It's symbolic to their cause to find it. They are searching other sites all over Europe for every last bar of Nazi gold. It will fund their terrorist activities in their quest to rebuild the Nazi...' He paused, searching for the right word. Then added bitterly, 'empire'.

They all fell silent.

'Right,' said Finn. 'So they're waiting for information about this gold and you don't know where it is? I mean, what the hell? This is a total nightmare. They'll just kill us all. No one's gonna rescue us now.'

'There must be some other way out of here,' Gus interrupted, feeling around in the dark.

'I moved it,' said Olde calmly. 'I'm so sorry Erik, my old

friend, for what you have suffered because of it.'

'Moved what?' said Finn.

'The gold. I moved it,' said Olde.

'What? How? I mean why?' said Erik.

'After we buried it in the cave, it pressed on me. I didn't want you to have the burden of it, knowing it was there. I admit, it was a foolish notion. And I felt it wasn't really a good enough hiding place. So I moved it bit by bit. Over a series of early morning fishing trips, I distributed it between two small caves in the fjord.'

'Olde, you're a legend!' said Finn.

'There are hundreds of caves in the fjord,' said Erik. 'Which ones?'

'I have no idea,' admitted Olde.

Finn let out a long exasperated sigh. 'I don't suppose just telling them to go and search all the caves is really going to wash?'

Silence filled the cellar.

'I still think there must be a way out of here,' said Gus, sounding positive. 'How many matches have you got left, Erik?'

'About six,' Erik said. 'Here,' he added despondently, 'take the box.'

Gus shuffled forward on his feet, keeping low, and struck a match. Storage boxes, tools and junk were propped up around the room. He began to move things to the side as he rummaged. The match died. He struck another, and Finn, seeing what his brother was doing shuffled over to him to help. As the match was held aloft, Finn moved the boxes away from the wall so that they could investigate further. As another match burnt out, another was lit. Olde and Erik fumbled to shift the boxes over, so that the boys could attempt to find an exit.

'What a lot of junk I've accumulated down here!' said Erik.

'I've not had a clear out for decades. If ever. I don't even remember what I've got. So it can't be very important. Just junk,' he repeated.

'Here,' said Finn, passing some shoe boxes and cartons over to Olde. 'Can you stack these?'

Olde obliged, feeling his way.

'Any luck?' he shouted over to Gus. 'How many matches are there left? Are we to die here, in the dark?'

His fingers slipped as he reached out for the next box and it dropped with a thud. As Gus lit the next match, Olde could make out the outline of an opened suitcase on the floor, its contents silhouetted. It was an old gramophone.

'It can't be,' whispered Olde. Now in the dark, he traced his fingers from the worn leather of the suitcase to the rippled turntable, the arm and then the sharp point of the needle. It seemed so familiar but it couldn't be—could it?

'Gus!' he said, his voice shrill with alarm and excitement. 'Come here! Don't light any more matches until you're right over here!'

'What is it, Olde?' asked Finn.

Gus crawled back over on his hands and knees, banging into boxes as he did so.

'What have you found?'

'Erik, you kept it?' murmured Olde, his mind flooding with memories.

'Kept what?' asked Erik, confused.

'My suitcase! The one I left here, in Norway, when I escaped!'

Chapter Forty-Three

The Suitcase
Norway 2014

There were two matches left.

Gus lit the first one, and sure enough, the old gramophone glimmered out from the darkness. Olde reached for the lid and retrieved the records tucked inside. He lifted one out and placed it on the turntable. Then he fumbled with the knobs and wound the handle on the side, just as the flame of the match slipped away once more. But Olde's fingers knew their way around the gramophone as though no time had passed at all. He gently moved the arm over, and with a familiar crackle the soaring sound of jazz clarinet filled the darkness.

'*Wang Wang Blues*!' laughed Olde. 'Benny Goodman.'

They sat for a moment, absorbing the music in Erik's dark, musty cellar.

'I remember the first time I ever heard this,' said Erik. 'It was outside your hut out there in the woods. The night the Nazis hid that gold in the cave.'

There was a momentary pause. Olde's mind awakened with the music. Memories buried deep were surfacing with every toe-tapping beat.

As the music drew to an end, he exclaimed excitedly, 'Gus, light the last match.'

'Are you sure, Olde,' asked Gus. 'Why?'

'Just do it,' said Olde firmly. 'Trust me,' he added. 'And hold it close. I'd completely forgotten until now; this suitcase has a secret compartment! I used it to smuggle the radio for the Resistance!'

Olde put his fingers out to the gramophone so that he'd be ready. He heard the strike of the match and at the birth of the tiny flame, he set to work with Gus crouched close by. Olde fumbled for a tiny catch on the side and, with a click, felt for another one. With both catches released, he lifted out the entire base to reveal a secret compartment below.

He reached his hand inside and lifted out a folded piece of paper. Olde quickly opened it out to reveal a map.

'What's that?' asked Gus, straining to see.

'It's a... a map,' said Olde, stuttering with excitement. 'A map of the fjord.'

'So?' said Finn. 'Why would you need to hide that?'

'Because, my boy, I hid it 70 years ago after carefully marking on the location of each cave!'

'Where you hid the gold?' said Finn.

'Yes,' said Olde, holding the map close to his face. The match was about to fizzle out to a black shard, but just before it did, Olde recognised two marks on the map. Two caves were highlighted, their exact locations in startling detail. But darkness enveloped them again and the miniature outline of the fjord was gone.

'But if you moved it, why write down where you hid it? asked Gus.

'The gold belonged to the Jewish people,' Olde explained. 'It was snatched from them before they were murdered. Their jewellery, their wedding rings, their teeth even. Melted down and stamped with the Nazi emblem. I suppose I thought that maybe, once the war was over and the Nazis were quashed, that it could somehow be returned to their relatives or... I don't know. But over time, I moved on. I thought it was probably best left undiscovered where it couldn't easily fall into the wrong hands. Along with the gold, I buried the memory of it. Like I tried to bury the memories of everything else that happened during the war.'

'So what do we do now?' said Gus. 'Risk our lives by not telling those terrorists upstairs about this?'

It was too late for discussions. Above their heads, the trap door was flung open sending light shooting down, illuminating the jumbled mess below. Before they had time to think, footsteps thundered down the stairs and Frederick appeared waving his gun. He immediately hauled Olde to his feet, still clutching the map, and along with Finn and Gus they were hustled back up the stairs to the kitchen. Frederick returned for Erik who was also brought blinking and shocked into the dazzling daylight.

Frederick snatched the map out of Olde's hand and passed it to Kristoffer.

'It couldn't have worked out better really, could it, gentlemen?' he sneered. 'Did you think we wouldn't be listening in to your conversation?'

He signalled to a laptop which sat on the kitchen table.

'Amazing technology these days,' he added. 'There aren't any rats in that cellar, but there are a few bugs!' He let out a cackle at his own joke. Gus, Finn and Olde passed a look to each other. Olde shook his head in exasperation at their own obvious mistake.

'So, the map,' he said, passing it over to Frederick, 'will lead us straight there? But we'll bring you all along with us for the ride,' added Kristoffer.

'Let everyone go!' shouted Olde. 'It's me you want, not

them. Let them go.'

'No, Olde!' blurted Finn.

'Oh don't worry,' said Kristoffer. 'All in good time, gentlemen. I have no intention of letting you go. I need you to help load up the gold. Then, and only then, you will be disposed of.'

CHAPTER FORTY-FOUR

Gold Hunt
NORWAY 2014

Finn hadn't thought much about caves before. There were many in Shetland. The main one that tourists and geologists always wanted to visit was carved out of the black cliffs at Eshaness. But the only cave he could think of that had any significance in his life was one his dad had taken him and Gus to as young boys to fish for crabs. Inside the damp rocky cell, they would tie a mussel to a long piece of string to dangle into a large, dark rock pool. And sometimes, if they were lucky, when they pulled the string back out, there was a tiny crab, its sharp pincers clamped tightly around the soft mussel. This was no crab hunt he was on now. He stared out along the craggy coastline; his hands were tied tightly behind his back.

Back on *The Northern Light*, now under Nazi control, they slowly wound their way back up the fjord. There was a lot of babble in Norwegian between Kristoffer and Frederick. They were poring over Olde's map and using a GPS machine to pinpoint the locations.

'They think they've found the first cave,' translated Erik. Sure enough, the boat now pulled up close to a rocky coastline.

'Well?' said Kristoffer, turning to face his prisoners, who were all tied up at the stern of the boat. 'Does this bring back any memories?' He spoke directly to Olde. 'Whereabouts exactly do you think you might have hidden a load of gold in here? Any clues, traitor?'

'It was seventy years ago,' Olde sighed wearily. 'But I was alone, so it can't have been too arduous.'

The anchor was lowered and Frederick, now wearing a head torch, leapt down into the dinghy which had been towed behind the fishing boat. He lifted out a metal detector, a pick axe and some shovels, and signalled for Gus and Finn to clamber down too. This was awkward as their hands had been tightly bound with rope. Then the dinghy took them closer to shore. The tide was out, but in a few hours the cave would be engulfed in water and inaccessible. Now out of the dinghy, they waded up to a small beach, with fresh, smooth white sand and the opening of a rough cavern beyond. It was small and they had to crouch to get in, but once inside it opened out and at points they could easily stand. The metal detector was turned on and they all watched and listened as it was scanned around in the semi darkness. Crouching down and looking out towards daylight, Finn could make out Olde and Erik bobbing at the stern of the boat as if they were out for a spot of fishing. Except there was Kristoffer watching, menacingly, at the bow.

Frederick reached over to Gus and Finn. He untied them and pushed a shovel into their hands.

'Don't think of using these as weapons, boys,' he said, reaching into his jacket to reveal his gun.

Finn moved his elbow down to his pocket. He too had a gun, he thought. But he had no idea how, or when, to use it. He was waiting for the right moment. But when would that be?

Blips and bleeps sounded from the detector.

'Check here!' yelled Frederick. 'It's not too deep, so use your hands first.'

Gus knelt down and scraped sand and rock away. In the light of the head torch he scooped and sifted with his fingers to find something. He clawed around at the base of the cave, then held up an object.

'This is what you found,' he said. Frederick snatched it and examined it closely.

'It's just a tin can,' he snapped. He scanned over the area again with the detector. But now it fell silent.

Frederick cursed and moved on. Once again there was a bleep. And again Gus and Finn were ordered to search, this time they found a hook of some description. This process seemed to go on forever. They accumulated a pile of junk including more fishing hooks, buttons and tin cans, even a bicycle wheel.

'The tide is coming in,' said Gus. The water was beginning to lap into the cave now. 'We'll need to work fast unless we want to be working underwater.'

'We have wet suits,' snapped Frederick. 'So that won't be a problem for you.'

Sharp words were yelled abruptly from outside the cave in Norwegian. Kristoffer was impatient.

Frederick shouted back. He began waving the detector again more urgently with low swings.

Frederick changed the dial on the controls. He was looking deeper now.

Finn wondered if he should seize his chance while Frederick was distracted. He slipped his hand into his pocket, reassuring himself that the gun was still there. His pulse raced. How would this unfold? Would he shoot, or would he just threaten? He felt for the trigger and pushed his fore and middle fingers inside the loop of cold metal. Could he aim at his legs, so as not to actually kill anyone? Killing someone was not something he could get his head around. His thumb rested on the hammer. Finn's hand trembled. He could feel it against his hip. His mouth felt dry. This was it. He gradually applied pressure down on the hammer and was about to whip the gun out when they all heard a low pulse: the detector started to bleep. Finn released his thumb. He took a deep breath and closed his eyes. Something washed over him. What was it?

Then he realised angrily: it was relief. He didn't have it in him. He was too much of a coward.

The detector gave a strong pulsating beat this time. It didn't waver as Frederick swept over a small space at the back of the cave. There were a number of large boulders over the spot, which Finn and Gus were now to ordered to move. They were unbearably heavy. But with great effort, they managed to shift them out of the way. Now with shovels, they were commanded to dig.

'There's nothing down here,' complained Gus, as they burrowed deeper into the sand.

'Dig!' snapped Frederick, looming overhead, giving Gus a cuff. But a flash of doubt passed over his face too. He snatched up the detector and waved it over the hole. The bleep was instant, loud and unmistakable.

'It's here,' he bellowed, and snatched the shovel from Finn who was floundering. Frederick gave him a sharp blow in the stomach to move him out of the way. Finn fell to the ground in pain. Gus immediately turned to his brother. And then there was a clang of metal on metal. Frederick fell to his knees and grabbed with his hands, frantically hauling out great handfuls of sand and with an almighty heave, he plucked a slab of sandy, but glittering, bullion out of its hiding place and lifted it high into the air.

'*Gold!*' Frederick shrieked. 'We've found the gold!'

CHAPTER FORTY-FIVE

Erik and Olde
NORWAY 2014

Finn lay doubled over, winded on the sandy bed of the cave. Even through his pain, he couldn't deny there was a certain thrill in seeing the gold bar held aloft. But this "treasure» was nothing to celebrate. And he was ashamed of himself for even taking any pleasure in their find.

Frederick quickly hauled up the bars, stopping every so often to examine the surface of the bullion. After one last scan around with the detector, he seemed satisfied that they were finished.

Finn was curled on the sandy bed of the cave. Frederick glared at him and gave him a swift kick in the groin. The pain now was unbearable. Tears swam in Finn's eyes. Gus let out a yell.

'Hey!' he yelled at Frederick. But the Nazi only laughed.

'Get this gold out to the boat. We're not done with you yet,' he yelled.

Finn and Gus reluctantly began to ferry the gold out to *The Northern Light* on the dinghy. Kristoffer snatched a bar and kissed its gleaming surface.

'At last!' he breathed. 'I've waited seventy years for this moment!'

Olde looked on despairingly. The gold stood for so much. A Nazi symbol of the destruction of his ancestry—turning Jews into gold to be hoarded or sold as a commodity: the funding of evil.

He looked away from Kristoffer in disgust.

Above, a sea eagle soared overhead, its yelps like a shriek of anguish.

Gus and Finn were ordered back into the boat, their hands once again bound tightly to the rails.

'I have no use for the old men; the boat can't take the weight. Not with all this,' said Kristoffer, his hands fanning over the bullion. 'Leave them in the cave. The tide will wash them away.'

'What?' shouted Gus. 'No!'

Frederick grabbed Erik and Olde and bundled them towards the side of the boat. With their hands tied together, they shuffled cautiously. With a sudden violent jerk, Erik caught his foot and fell at Gus's feet. His glasses fell from his face and slid to the floor. Gus instantly thrust himself forward to help. But with hands tied, he could do very little.

'*Sabotage*,' whispered Erik, staring desperately into Gus's eyes, his words barely audible above the curses and shouts of their captors and yelling from Finn. 'Engage in any act of sabotage if it's to further our cause. Look into yourself and find all the courage you can muster...' Then he added, 'Get rid of that gold, Gus. It's more important than the lives of two old men.'

'Move!' yelled Frederick, giving Erik a shove. And for good measure he stamped on Erik's glasses as he hauled him up.

Gus locked eyes with Erik as he was lifted away. Erik stared unblinking, as if willing Gus to grasp the magnitude of what he had said.

Frederick bundled Erik and Olde out into the dinghy, and once at the opening to the cave they were pushed stumbling and splashing clumsily inside.

'Olde!' shouted Finn, desperately, his voice breaking, 'NO!'

'You can't do that,' yelled Finn to Kristoffer. 'You can't just leave them there to drown.' Finn struggled violently. His face was red, veins protruding on his temples.

'Don't bother yourselves, boys,' said Kristoffer. 'We'll be finished with you too soon enough.' Then he let out a laugh.

Frederick appeared out of the mouth of the cave and jumped into the dinghy to join them on the boat.

'A fitting end!' declared Kristoffer in the direction of the cave, his voice echoing. 'To drown, in a small cavernous space. What a tribute to the one thousand Germans who died on the upturned *Tirpitz*. We're done here,' he said, turning to his grandson. And with that, the engine fired into life and the boat moved slowly away from the cave.

'No!' said Finn, staring into the face of his brother. 'Gus! We have to do something!' Tears were streaming down his face.

'There's nothing we can do, Finn,' Gus said loudly so that their captors would hear. Then he added quietly giving his brother a nod, 'Yet.' He twisted his head to look back at the cave. Finn could just make it out until it was lost in the rocks and formations of the coastline. Even if they could get back, would they ever find it? He looked up above the rocks and stared for something, anything distinctive that would lead them back there, but as they moved further away, the landscape merged into a moss-grey silhouette. High above on the rocks, twisted and gnarled, stood a dead tree, its branches still reaching out into the sky. Gus also fixed his eyes on it as the boat moved further and further into the expanse of the fjord. A large bird circled before swooping down to the old tree, where it disappeared into a clump of branches.

Finn wept. If he'd had the courage to use that gun in his pocket, maybe Olde would have been saved.

'I'm such a coward,' he mumbled softly.

He looked up to Frederick and Kristoffer who were in a state of triumph. They were laughing and joking. Every so often they would lift up a gold bar. Finn felt the urge to vomit. He thrust his head forward and threw up.

'It'll be okay,' Gus tried to soothe. But Finn wasn't convinced.

'No it won't! It won't! How can you stay so calm?'

Finn felt certain that they were all facing death. And as that reality formed in his mind, rage began to boil in his blood.

Olde and Erik, tied together, sitting back to back on the sandy floor of the cave, peered out through the rocky opening as the boat sped away. When it was merely a dot on the horizon, Erik finally spoke.

'So, my old friend,' he said. 'It has come to this.'

The water from the rising tide now lapped halfway up the cave towards them.

'Can I tell you something?' Olde began. 'I always feared this death. In fact, it has haunted my dreams now for nearly seventy years.'

Erik was silent.

'Those poor men on board *Tirpitz*,' Olde murmured. 'And of course your father. I never forgave myself for that. Remorse and guilt have been my closest friends since that time.'

As they sat in the darkness of the cave, the swirling water was filling the hole left by the stash of gold. With each fold of water, a bubbling cauldron frothed, fizzed in the sand and then emptied until it filled again once more.

Erik shook his head. 'Hans,' he said. 'Do you remember what you told me back then?' He turned his head around. 'You said we had to consider the bigger picture. And that's exactly what we all did; it was the spirit of the war. Times were very different. And we pulled together.' He was quiet for a minute. 'Why was it, my dear friend, that you never made contact with me?' He paused. 'You never wrote.'

'I couldn't reveal my location,' said Olde. 'The Germans were still intercepting mail and I couldn't reveal any of the work that was still going on with the Resistance in Shetland, as I still worked very closely with them. After the war, I suppose

I tried to forget. To move on. And to create a whole new identity.' He paused and then added, 'I am so sorry, Erik. It was shameful really.'

'There is nothing to forgive,' said Erik. 'Nothing at all. You came! You came all the way from Shetland. All the way up here to find me!'

'Not that it has done us much good,' whispered Olde.

They sat in silence as the freezing water crept nearer and lapped gently at their feet.

Chapter Forty-Six

Finn and Gus
Norway 2014

'Sabotage,' whispered Gus. It was so quietly murmured that it could have been a sigh or a whistle through his teeth.

Finn rubbed his swollen eyes and turned his head round to look at his brother who stared wistfully out across the fjord. Gus sat silently now as if he'd never uttered a word. All Finn could hear was the steady pulse of this breath. He wondered what Gus was planning. They were being watched closely; it was too dangerous to say or do anything. But his brother's face was gripped—taut and intense. Time wasn't on their side, so it had to be something fast, instant. Something devastating. He still had the gun. When the moment came, they would have to act without doubt or hesitation. He closed his eyes tight, listening to the thrum of the engine. When he opened his eyes, Gus glanced over. Momentarily, they locked eyes, and for a second, it was as if somehow they understood: this wasn't over.

'Here!' shouted a voice. Frederick had identified the other cave. This looked similar to the first, except the tide had already covered the entrance. The water would be creeping nearer to Olde and Erik.

Once again, they climbed into the dinghy and transferred the metal detector and tools. Soon they were heading away from *The Northern Light* to the cave.

The search this time was much faster. The detector had

been set to discover deeper items, and very quickly Finn and Gus were instructed to dig. There was a shout as the bars were discovered—the stash here was bigger. There were at least fifty bars to shift. And so the brothers set off, escorted each time by the gun-wielding Frederick back to unload to Kristoffer at the boat. On the final journey, all three of them were crowded onto the dinghy with the last stash.

'I need to use the loo,' Gus said desperately, as they began handing over the bars of gold onto *The Northern Light*. Finn glared at his brother.

'Use the sea!' said Frederick curtly.

'It's not that,' Gus replied, trying to look bashful. 'You know what it's like, when you've got to go, you've got to go. It's braaly urgent. I mean, you know,' he wittered on, 'I can't hold on any longer—I've been struggling as it is.'

'Whatever,' snapped Kristoffer. 'Get on with it. And be quick about it.'

Gus clambered up and over into the boat, leaving Finn to shift the last of the gold. Before he slipped over the barrier, he shot a look to his brother. It was the kind of loaded look that only siblings would understand. He dashed quickly into the wheelhouse and down the narrow staircase below deck. Finn knew, in that moment, to be ready.

'You!' snapped Frederick, to Finn. 'Get a move on!'

Climbing back on board *The Northern Light*, Finn dutifully lifted and carried the last of the gold carefully over to the large pile which had accumulated on the starboard side of the boat. Kristoffer now counted the bars; it was a considerable haul.

'We shouldn't put it all on one side,' Finn said sharply to Frederick.

'Shut up!' he snapped, glowering towards the wheelhouse, clearly impatient for Gus to reappear.

'But if we...' continued Finn. But Frederick marched inside, ordering Gus to get a move on. Finn could see him drop down the stairs.

'Get up here, pathetic scum!' Frederick's voice commanded. Finn could sense that something pretty awful was about to happen. Instinctively he reached his hand into his pocket for the gun.

Gus was being hauled on deck. He was flung onto the floor. Frederick kicked him hard in the groin. Gus let out a yowl in pain and Frederick booted him again for good measure.

'Don't like hard work, eh? Trying to take a little nap down there, were we?'

He lifted his boot again and with unflinching speed kicked him hard in the stomach. Gus, momentarily passed out.

Kristoffer came over to join them. 'Finish him,' he said casually, as though his patience had simply drained away. 'And his brother. We have no need for them now. We have all the gold. We can be on our way to the others without this dead weight.'

There was a moment of hesitation. Frederick shot a look to his grandfather. A flash of doubt, or was it disbelief, had passed over him.

'Finish him!' ordered Kristoffer. 'And the other one too.'

Finn cried out, panic-stricken. Terror made him freeze momentarily at what was about to happen.

Frederick reached into his jacket and pulled out the gun. But before he could even raise the weapon there was an angry shout.

'Stop right there,' interrupted Finn, pointing his revolver. Rage had overtaken fear. He was in control and ready to fight for their lives.

Kristoffer and Frederick looked at Finn in surprise. But Kristoffer, undeterred by Finn's gun, let out a scornful laugh.

'Put that ancient thing down, you stupid little boy,' he sneered, edging closer. But his grandson looked less confident. He clearly recognised the change in Finn.

'Drop the gun!' Finn yelled, pointing at Frederick.

'Shoot him!' commanded Kristoffer. But before Frederick had time, a shot rang out. Finn had pulled the trigger.

Frederick shrieked in pain, clutching his shoulder. His gun tumbled out of his fingers and dropped to the ground, sliding along the deck where it slipped through the barrier and into the water.

In the confusion, Finn hadn't expected Kristoffer to lunge for him. There was no time to re-cock the revolver before the old man threw him backwards, crashing to the ground. Finn was horrified at the extraordinary strength of the old man, but still he didn't release the gun from his grip. Kristoffer now grasped one bony hand around his throat, pinning him to the deck while the other hand grappled to get the weapon; Finn couldn't breathe. Panic and terror consumed him. He clawed at Kristoffer's arm with his free hand, and kicked out his legs, as the pressure on his gullet increased. Black spots now spawned and dispersed in front of the image of Kristoffer, teeth bared, eyes red with fury, focussing on his victim with such ferocity that Finn began to accept it was over. The black spots now started to merge and to join together. He stopped struggling, and his hands and legs went limp.

CHAPTER FORTY-SEVEN

The Final Battle

NORWAY 2014

Finn could sense he was drifting in and out of consciousness. The blurry image of Kristoffer on his haunches, leaning over him, flashed before his eyes like some terrible nightmare. He could feel himself slipping into endless darkness when from somewhere he heard a voice, wild with fury, like an animal. And then he felt the pressure on his throat release. He instinctively rolled over and heaved and coughed as air once more filled his lungs.

Still injured with blood smeared across his face and hands tightly gripped, Gus had hauled himself up and had lunged awkwardly and violently at Kristoffer.

'Get off my brother!' he roared in a voice that Finn barely recognised.

Kristoffer fell heavily, hitting his head on a crate. Blood oozed down his face but his eyes filled with evil mockery.

Back on his feet, Gus grabbed his brother and pulled him towards the stern of the boat. But now Kristoffer was back up too. Finn lifted up the gun in his now free hand and re-cocked it, aiming at the old man. Then Frederick with his bleeding shoulder appeared. Although injured, he still looked capable of causing harm, like a wounded rhinoceros, angry and determined. He joined his grandfather approaching the two boys. They continued to back away. Finn squeezed the trigger, but all that followed was a dull click. He tried to reload, and fire. Nothing. There were no more bullets. Had there really only been one bullet?

'In the dinghy, now!' yelled Gus scrambling over the barrier. 'We have to get back to Olde!'

'What?' said Finn—confusion reigned in his mind. How could his brother be letting them go like this? On their boat too? But Kristoffer and Frederick were now moving swiftly towards them.

'Let them go,' Gus repeated, through gritted teeth, clambering into the dinghy.

'What about the boat?' Finn said faltering. 'We can't let them take the boat!'

'Finn!' barked Gus. 'Do it! We've no choice!' He pulled on the motor. 'Now Finn. NOW!'

Kristoffer tried to grab Finn as he swung over the barrier. He wasn't quite fast enough, but his grandson was, and held onto Finn by his arm and hauled him back up. In one swift motion, Gus stood up and gave Frederick a mighty thud with an oar, directly on his injured shoulder. Frederick howled in pain and Finn dropped into the dinghy below—just as it began to move.

The gap between them and *The Northern Light* grew fast as they sped back up the fjord.

Kristoffer stood on the deck.

'Thank you very much for your time, gentlemen,' he shouted scornfully. 'It's been a pleasure!' his voice echoed. Then he reached out a hand sharply, making the Nazi salute. 'The old men will be dead by now!' He added. 'You are wasting your time. And we will find you. We will hunt you down! Even if it takes a lifetime!'

There was a shift in the engine's tone as *The Northern Light* set off into the fjord. The outstretched hand of Kristoffer became smaller as the boat sailed further and further away, leaving behind only a white stream of froth on the surface of the water.

'What have we done?' said Finn, still out of breath. 'They're getting away!'

'They'll not get far,' remarked Gus, wiping the blood from his head on his sleeve.

Finn shot a look to his brother.

'Sabotage,' Gus said. His eyes remained fixed on their trusty fishing boat.

As they navigated themselves back up the fjord, they looked out to watch *The Northern Light*. Now, some way off in the distance, it had stopped moving. Something wasn't right. It seemed to be a little off-kilter.

'What did you do?' asked Finn.

'I just made a few minor adjustments,' he said. 'I smashed the bilge pump and that ropey pipe into the toilet. That was all I managed before I heard Frederick coming down the ladder. I had to shoot into the bunk room so it looked like I'd been having a nap. It should be enough though.'

Finn was impressed at his brother's quick thinking.

'They never heard anything over the noise of the engine,' said Gus. 'And they clearly have no idea about boats, so with the bilge alarm going off, well, they won't know where to start.'

Finn nodded, absorbing this information.

'I don't think dad will be best pleased,' Gus added.

A look of horror flashed over Finn's face—a dawning of understanding. 'You mean...?' he gasped.

'She's going down, Finn. She's going down,' confirmed Gus.

They sat quietly.

'Sometimes Finn, you have to look at the bigger picture,' said Gus, turning his head to scan the coastline. 'But there's no time to discuss it any more,' Gus said firmly. 'We've got to find Olde and Erik! Before it's too late!'

Chapter Forty-Eight

The Sea Eagle
Norway 1944

'How the hell are we going to find them?' said Finn, scouring the coastline. 'It's impossible—everything looks the same!'

'How long do you reckon since we left?' asked Gus. 'Two hours maybe?'

Finn nodded, still staring wildly along the rocks. 'Aye, yeah, something like that. Nothing looks the same now. The tide has come right in. This is useless, Gus!'

'It's that way,' said Gus, with a shout. Finn glanced at his brother who was looking up towards the sky. 'I recognise the shapes of the rocks. But we need to look out for sea eagles.'

'Can't we make this thing go any faster?' snapped Finn, willing the outboard motor to break free from its spluttering into a throaty roar. But the spluttering became more pronounced. Finn glanced nervously at his brother. 'That doesn't sound too healthy. It's not going to make it,' he wailed.

The dinghy began to slow as the outboard choked and heaved. Then it was silent. And there they sat, gently rocking on the tide.

'Damn it!' shouted Finn, tugging on the cord helplessly. But it was no use.

Gus pulled out the two oars tucked under the seats and awkwardly passed one to his brother.

'There's nothing else for it!' he said. 'No time for hesitation or self-pity.'

With one oar each, working at full pelt, they dragged the dinghy onwards, still scanning the coastline.

'We're never going to make it!' wailed Finn, exasperated by the slow progress they were making.

'There!' exclaimed Gus. 'Look up!'

The boys strained their heads. A large bird circled against the pale blue sky. Broad and majestic, its white tail and yellow beak flashed in the sun.

'It's a sea eagle!' confirmed Gus. 'And there's the tree—the nest! The cave was directly below it!'

It took all their strength to row at speed towards the cave. As they approached the rocky coastline, it did seem to look familiar. The water level was much higher now and this time they were able to row directly inside the cave.

'Olde?' cried out Finn.

'Erik!' hollered Gus.

It was pitch black and their voices echoed strangely. Then a small, weak voice answered back, 'Boys?'

It was Olde.

The freezing water was now around the waists of Erik and Olde, still tied together in the darkness.

Finn and Gus leapt out of the boat and waded as fast as they could towards the two old men.

'We thought you'd never come,' said Erik, his teeth chattering, barely able to talk. 'Are you both okay?' His speech was laboured and hoarse.

'Don't worry about us, we're fine,' said Gus, his voice shaking with emotion. 'Save your energy, don't talk anymore,' he added with a wink.

Lifting one man each, Finn and Gus raised Erik and Olde to their feet and hauled them over to the dinghy. Instinctively, they stripped off their own jumpers and wrapped them tightly around them. Both Erik and Olde were shivering uncontrollably. Once safely in the boat, Finn worked on the knot of the rope binding the two old men together.

'We've got to get them ashore and warm as quickly as possible,' said Gus to his brother, beginning to turn the boat with his one oar. With the knot untied, Finn joined him and they began to row with a renewed sense of urgency and energy back out into the fjord.

'What happened?' murmured Olde, rubbing his wrists, as the dinghy pushed its way out into the fjord.

'Look!' said Finn, pointing in the direction of *The Northern Light*.

Although a good way off, they could clearly make out the shape of their fishing boat in the distance tipped on her side. They stopped rowing and in the lull and lap of the water, they watched as their boat gradually slipped below the surface in front of their eyes.

'Good God!' said Olde, his voice strained. 'Is that ours?'

'Yes,' said Gus.

'They'd put all the gold on the starboard side. I did try to explain that it wasn't the best plan,' said Finn. 'It's tipped them over!'

'Yeah, but they probably weren't expecting there to be a hole in the hull,' added Gus.

Within minutes, the outline of the boat was gone.

'All that gold will now be sinking to the very bottom of the fjord,' said Erik. 'It's so deep down there, it'll be gone forever.'

'Best place for it,' added Olde.

Finn and Gus eased the oars into a steady rhythm, taking Olde and Erik to safety.

Somewhere above their heads, there was a screech, proud and triumphant. The sea eagle soared past, its wings outstretched, a silhouette against the sky.

Chapter Forty-Nine

Havørn

Lerwick, The Shetland Islands 2014

Finn bounded up the steps to Bay View Care Home.

'Morning, Joan!' he called to the lady on the desk.

'Back again, Finn?' she said.

'Yup,' replied Finn. 'But today's a wee bit of a special one!'

'You can say that again!' said Joan with a chuckle.

Without any hesitation, Finn headed straight for the main sitting room with big strides.

'Well, Olde?' he said, barely able to contain his excitement. A few of the other residents looked up. 'Are you ready?'

Olde put down his paper and gave his great grandson a beaming smile.

'Woah!' said Finn, glancing at his great-grandfather's outfit. 'Looking sharp there, dude!'

Olde was dressed in a blazer and tie.

'Thought I ought to make an effort,' he said. 'Where's Gus?'

'He's outside in the van,' he said, and checked his watch. 'We need to get going. The ceremony starts in twenty minutes.'

Finn helped Olde to his feet. With arms locked, they made their way to the front desk.

'That's us just off, Joan,' said Olde.

'Hold it there, mister,' shouted a voice behind them.

Olde and Finn froze. It was Heather, the care assistant.

'Now, the last time you went out for a "wee jaunt" you ended up in Norway! Remember?' But her face broke into a large smile. She straightened Olde's tie.

'No funny business this time!' she said, gently nudging Olde. 'No crazy adventures! No more saving the world for you, superman!'

'Absolutely!' smiled Olde.

'I promise to bring him right back after the ceremony,' said Finn, with a straight face.

'Well, maybe not *right* back,' added Olde, with a wink.

Gus was waiting outside, the engine running, ready to set off once again for the harbour.

'Gus, my boy!' said Olde, as he snapped on his seatbelt. 'Not too fast now. I mean, I am an old man after all!'

'Yeah, right,' said Gus, with a grin.

'Wait a minute,' Olde said.

'What's up?' asked Gus.

'Erik came by to visit me earlier.'

'Yeah, we know,' said Finn. 'We dropped him off. Why?'

'He wanted to fill me in. And well, now I'm doing the same for you.'

'Spit it out, Olde, we've not got long.'

'They...' he stammered. 'The authorities in Norway, they've, em, found a body. In the fjord.'

'But it was weeks ago!' said Finn.

'Well that can sometimes happen,' said Olde. 'With the tide and everything. It was Kristoffer's. They think he probably drowned trying to hold onto the gold in that freezing water. The gold is now at the bottom of the fjord, by the way. And it's been kept under wraps that there ever was any gold discovered to avoid the place being inundated with divers. So that bit is still hush-hush, as it were.'

'Okay,' said Gus. 'But what about that evil grandson, Frederick?'

'No sign yet,' said Olde. 'Which is peculiar. But, there we go.'

'He was maybe washed out to sea, you know,' added Finn.

'That water was too cold for survival, surely? And he had a bullet in his shoulder.'

Finn kept his thoughts to himself that perhaps somehow Frederick was still out there. Saying anything out loud would only serve to feed the fear.

'Well, it's over,' said Olde. 'Let's get going and put all this behind us!'

Gus slipped the van into gear and pulled out of the car park and they headed down towards the harbour once more. But this time, their arrival wasn't draped in mystery and plans for escape. This time they were greeted by hundreds of people. Locals who had come out in force, beaming and waving as Olde, Finn and Gus climbed out of the van. Metres of bunting zigzagged overhead, the little coloured triangles flapping wildly. Erik, who had been standing in a group of smartly dressed veterans, stepped forward and shook Olde, Finn and Gus enthusiastically by the hand. Cameras flashed from the crowd. Finn and Gus waved over at their dad and grandmother.

They were ushered over to sit on seats reserved for them on a little platform. A microphone whistled as the Convenor of the Shetland Islands stood up.

'There are no words,' he began, 'to describe the bravery of these four men sitting here.' He turned and looked at Finn, Gus, Olde and Erik. 'Erik, here from Norway, and of course our honorary Shetlander Hans, tackled the Nazis seventy years ago. And spanning the decades and indeed generations, that spirit—that courage—has endured, being passed on to young Finn and Gus. In squaring up to the terrorist group that threatened your lives and our peaceful societies here, and in Norway and beyond, you have saved countless lives. And proved that good really can conquer evil.' He paused and added warmly, 'We thank you.'

There was a ripple of applause.

'The bond we Shetlanders have with Norway has now been

forever sealed by your extraordinary bravery,' he continued. 'In recognition of this, a fund was set up to replace the fishing boat lost to the depths of the fjord in northern Norway. The response, not only in Norway and Scotland, but across the world on hearing of your brave exploits has been utterly overwhelming. Enough was raised for this beauty here,' he smiled broadly, directing his hands to the dock. There, on the slipway, sat a magnificent red fishing boat, swathed in bunting and red ribbon; the Saltire and Norwegian flag were prominent on poles either side.

'Erik? I wonder if you would you do the honours?' asked the Convenor.

Erik stood up and walked towards the fishing boat. A bottle of whisky hung on a rope.

'It gives me great pleasure to name this boat *Havørn*,' Erik announced proudly, then he quickly translated: 'The Sea Eagle. May her voyages be safe and fruitful. And for her sake, I hope she doesn't have to endure many long journeys to North Norway! Although she will always, always be welcome!'

A great roar of applause echoed round the harbour as Erik released the whisky and it shattered against the bow of the red fishing boat. And slowly, majestically, she edged forward down the slipway.

'Do you fancy a wee spin in her?' said Gus, turning to Olde who clapped enthusiastically, wiping a tear from his face.

'C'mon Olde!' said Finn. 'For old times' sake! We'll not go far,' he added with a wink.

Olde reached up and put his arms around his great-grandsons.

'I wouldn't miss it for the world!' he chuckled. 'Not for the world.'

THE END

Glossary

billets: accommodation for soldiers or military people

braaly: Shetland dialect meaning quite or fairly

fjord: a long narrow inlet of the sea

Gestapo: the secret police force during the Nazi regime

gramophone: old fashioned type of record player

Neo-Nazi: modern or more recent movements of the Nazi party

Nazi: a member of the National Socialist German Workers' Party, which controlled Germany under Adolf Hitler. Or a person who holds similar views.

peerie: Shetland dialect meaning small

radar: a device for tracking distant objects by bouncing high-frequency radio pulses off them

squall line: a line of thunderstorms along a cold front, with severe weather conditions such as high winds, hail and rain.

stockfish: air-dried fish

SS: Nazi security police

toon: Shetland dialect for a town—referring here to Lerwick, Shetland's capital.

Author's Note

The battleship *Tirpitz* was successfully bombed as part of Operation Catechism, after many failed attempts, on the 12th November 1944. Around 1000 Germans lost their lives.

I've always had an interest in *Tirpitz*, thanks to my dad! He read many books about it throughout my childhood and to be honest, I thought the name itself was intriguing. Then, a few years ago, I watched documentary called *The Dambusters' Great Escape* on Channel 4. In it, historian Patrick Bishop explained how the battleship *Tirpitz* finally met her end in Northern Norway. Bishop met with a man called Sander Pettersen who had worked in a radar station during the war, when Norway was under Nazi occupation. The German radar operator retrieved a tiny silk Union Jack flag from his cigarette case, thus revealing he was working against his own people. Pettersen suggested that the German had withheld vital information from the airbase at Bardufoss, giving the British bombers the time to bomb *Tirpitz* free from attack by the German fighter planes.

This story sparked something within me: an idea to fictionalise his story. That perhaps this radar operator escaped to Shetland! So I began to read about the 'Shetland Bus' and all about *Tirpitz*. Two books fascinated me: *Target Tirpitz* by Patrick Bishop and *The Shetland Bus* by David Haworth. They are well worth exploring.

I slowly began to weave a fictional story into the factual history. Having family in Northern Norway meant I could research the area, as well as fascinating sub plots, like the plight of the Sami people.

It has been a joy to research. Thanks for sharing your story Mr. Pettersen and for giving me your blessing to use your 'cigarette case' memory within the book.

The story of Norway and of the bravery of everyday Norwegians during WW2 is remarkable. I hope this story does them proud!

Michelle

Acknowledgements

I couldn't have written the story without the help of some wonderful people. First of all, I owe a huge debt of thanks to my sister-in-law Lindis Sloan, a proud Norwegian, her knowledge is encyclopaedic. I consulted her on all things from history, culture, rural issues to reindeer husbandry and dried fish! Thank you Lindis. I hope I've done you proud.

Robert Watret gave me a fantastic insight to life on board a fishing boat. It gave me many laughs and I have a new found respect for those who spend days and nights out in the North Sea.

John Down discussed the sail from Shetland to Norway with me. He gave me so much information and ideas on the practicality of that journey. Thanks John—you inspired many of the key chapters at sea. And thanks to his wife Marit too for insights into life in Norway during the war.

Thanks to Jacqui Clark, Kirsten Leask and Jane Bray for help with Shetland dialect.

Thanks also to Melanie Henderson from Lerwick Harbour.

Thank you to Leif Pareli, Curator of the Sami Collection, The Norwegian Museum of Cultural History

Thanks to Kay MacIntyre for your absolute support and enthusiastic early editing. And Alasdair, for giving me an interest in *Tirpitz* since childhood!

Thanks to Helen, Anne, and also John Fulton, for all your support and encouragement. "Clan Cranachan" is a wonderful thing!

And to Donald who has been a patient sounding board and gentle critic from the outset. I would never have had the confidence to even tackle this book without your support and belief.

About the Author

Michelle lives in sunny Broughty Ferry, Dundee with her husband, three children, Lola the feisty cat and Scruff the daft mutt.

She trained as a Primary Teacher and worked for many years in Edinburgh, before indulging her love of all things theatrical by returning to university to study Drama.

After dabbling in performance art in Glasgow, and starring in a one woman show in Edinburgh, Michelle finally settled on a specialty in Arts Journalism and developed a new, unknown passion for writing!

She is also the author of *The Fourth Bonniest Baby in Dundee.*

You can contact Michelle at www.michellesloan.co.uk or on Twitter @michlsloan

yesteryear

Also available in the Yesteryear Series

The Beast on the Broch
by John K. Fulton

Scotland, 799 AD. Talorca befriends a strange Pictish beast; together, they fight off Viking raiders.

Fir for Luck
by Barbara Henderson

The heart-wrenching tale of a girl's courage to save her village from the Highland Clearances.

To download free reading resources and lesson plans to accompany all of our books please visit:

www.cranachanpublishing.co.uk

Thank You for Reading

As we say at Cranachan,
'the proof of the pudding is in the reading'
and we hope that you enjoyed *The Revenge of Tirpitz.*

Please tell all your friends and tweet us with your
#therevengeoftirpitz feedback, or better still, write an
online review to help spread the word!

We only publish books which excite and inspire us, so if
you'd like to experience other unique and
thought-provoking books, please visit our website:

cranachanpublishing.co.uk

and follow us
@cranachanbooks
for news of our forthcoming titles.

cranachan

Lightning Source UK Ltd.
Milton Keynes UK
UKOW06f0937160816

280796UK00017B/343/P